WILD, WILD, DUKE

COPYRIGHT

Wild, Wild, Duke
The Wayward Yorks, Book 3
Copyright © 2023 by Tamara Gill
Cover Art by Wicked Smart Designs
Editor Grace Bradley Editing, LLC

ISBN: 978-0-6458465-8-4

CHAPTER
ONE

K ate stared at the Duke of Montague and could not reconcile that the gentleman who sat before her, a brooding and bullying beast, was the same man who had tempted her heart several years before.

His cold, calculated tone grated on emotions that lingered after the death of her husband a year before.

"A thousand pounds," she repeated, unable to comprehend the sum of debt her husband was in with His Grace. How had George come to owe so much? She knew he enjoyed a night or two at his clubs or gaming hells, but a thousand pounds? How was one ever to repay His Grace?

The duke leaned into the wingback chair, folding his legs as if the amount did not signify to him, but of course, it did. He would not be here in her home, asking her to pay it back if it did not.

"I will require time to settle it, Your Grace. I'm unsure how to deduct such an amount from my son's inheritance. I will have to consult my steward on our financial position."

"You may do as you wish, but I have waited over a year already to have this amount paid back and now no longer

1

wish to." He paused and met her eyes. No ounce of compassion or regret stared back at her. But she supposed that was to be expected after all the time that had passed since her first Season. Whatever they may have had, if anything, before she married Lord Brassel was long gone.

"Your steward will guide you, and I'm certain you'll be able to settle the amount within the week."

"The week." Kate slumped into the chair across from him, biting her lip to stop the tears that threatened. "Can you not give me more time than that? You have waited a year already. What is a fortnight at least more?"

"More time than I need to grant." The stony facade he set on his features eased a little, and for the first time in years, she saw a flicker of the man she had once known. "I do not demand the money out of spite or malicious intent. George was one of my closest friends, and I will forever miss him, but he was also lax in his honor. He promised me he would pay within a week of losing the money, and a year later, I'm still waiting. I am sorry for your loss, but I'm leaving for my Scottish estate soon and wish to have all my affairs here in town tidied up. I'm not certain when I shall return."

Kate nodded, hoping the steward could help her as quickly as the duke wished. She met his eyes and wondered for a moment what would have happened had she promenaded with His Grace as he had asked her to. Of course, she had attended Hyde Park as arranged, but instead of the duke arriving to escort her, Lord Brassel had instead, and the rest was a whirlwind of flattery and flowers that ended with an understanding before she knew it.

"The Wild Wolfe of London is leaving?" The words slipped from her lips before she could rip them back. His eyes narrowed, but instead of denying the name synonymous with him, he merely cocked his lips into a wicked grin and nodded.

"One must hang up his title at some point, but alas, my departure is not permanent. However, my travels to Scotland are tedious and lengthy. My estate is situated in the Highlands, so I do not wish to be rushing up there merely to return here before I must."

Kate couldn't help but wonder if a woman was part of why he was traveling so far north. Maybe he had a sweetheart hidden away all these years whom he was finally going to propose to? It would not be the first time such a thing occurred, but something told her His Grace was not so romantic, or the marrying kind.

Far from it, considering what he demanded from her this day.

"So you'll be leaving before the Season has finished. I'm sure many hearts will break, Your Grace."

He shrugged and did not recognize her attempt to lighten the mood. She had been hoping that he might change his mind if he could feel a little pity for her and this situation. Forgive the debt, or let her pay it off over time.

"I do not care for the ladies of the *ton*, Lady Brassel. My being here, demanding a debt to be paid, is proof of that. I am, of course, like you, part of the upper echelons of society, but I do not care for it like you do. I find the women most unpredictable, and that is nothing I want to associate with."

Kate gaped and, realizing such a fact, snapped her mouth closed. Was his thinly veiled barb aimed at her? Was he generalizing his statement but meaning her instead?

He had a lot of gall, considering he was the one who stood her up at the park all those years ago—he had sent his best friend in his stead when he had not wanted to tell her himself that he was no longer interested in promenading. She would not have been offended had he been honest, maybe slightly disappointed, but nothing more.

The cur.

"I'm meeting my steward today, so you're fortunate in that at least," she said, standing and wanting to end this farce of a meeting. His Grace had made it clear that their friendship was long over, and George's demise only finalized that fact. "Good day to you, Your Grace."

He stood, towering over her yet again, and bowed. "Lady Brassel, a pleasure as always."

W olfe strode from the room and fought the urge to glance back at Lady Brassel, Kate as he once had been at liberty to call her. Before his closest friend, Lord Brassel, thought to court her. Wolfe, the loyal friend to the very end, allowed him his way.

He stepped out onto the street and breathed deep the city air. How he valued London, the bustling streets, the variety of people, his life here, carefree, without obligations other than to himself and his tenants back at the county estate in Derbyshire.

All was perfect in his world, except the thousand pounds Brassel still owed him. It was a shame for Lady Brassel that he was not the forgiving type to forget the debt altogether, but he was not. He treasured few things in his life, but money was one of them, and he would get his blunt back, or unfortunately, her ladyship would feel the full wrath of the law.

He casually walked around Berkeley Square. The squeals of children playing on the greens and the nannies chasing them surrounded him. He stopped when a little boy, Brassel's son, he was sure, caught his attention. The lad had his mother's large blue eyes and dark hair. No doubt the boy would break hearts just as his mama had done during her youth.

Not that he could call her geriatric. She was far from a long-toothed, over-the-hill matron of the *ton*, but it soothed his pride a little that she was no longer a shining new debutante everyone wanted to court.

It pained him to realize how jaded he sounded. He pressed on, wanting to bathe before he met with his mistress Sally this evening. She, of course, would travel with him to Scotland, and he was looking forward to enjoying her without worrying about the *ton* seeing their every move.

Poor Sally was not so enthused. She was a woman who preferred London to Scotland and disliked the cold. But he had promised to keep her warm, and she would do well to remember who paid her wage.

The thought soured in his mind. Maybe he was jaded, a cold-hearted rogue that people thought him.

The Wild Wolfe of London.

He did not even know where the name originated or how Lady Brassel knew it. But then he supposed they had been friends once. Mayhap, she wished they still were...

In any case, a debt was a debt. He always paid his dues, and Brassel, dead or alive, would do so also. His widow had an heir, her future was secure, and it was only fitting he be paid after graciously allowing the IOU to stand for so long. He had nothing to feel guilty about.

So why did he feel like he'd just trampled a family pet with a carriage and, unsatisfied with that, went back and stomped on it to ensure it was dead...

TWO

"So you see, Lady Brassel, there is not enough cash flow on the books to allow such a loan to be repaid." Her steward studied the IOU George had penned to Duke Montague and resignedly shook his head. "I'm afraid you'll have to explain to the duke that the money is not there and will not be for several years. Although the country estate is profitable, those profits, I'm sorry to be the one to tell you this, my lady, Lord Brassel disbursed as soon and as often as he could, leaving very little to build up capital."

Kate swallowed the lump, and panic that rose in her throat over what Mr. Smith was saying regarding their financial position. "So, are you saying we have no money at all? Is there enough for us to live and remain in London to keep this property or others within the Brassel estate?"

The steward, an elderly gentleman, reached out and patted her hand. "There is enough to keep the houses going, and the staff paid along with the necessities like food and your ladyship enjoying the Season. But to give away a thousand pounds isn't feasible right now. By the time your son takes over the estate, he will have more than enough money to last him two lifetimes, but right now, there must be economies, and paying back a gambling debt isn't feasible."

Could this week get any worse? First, hearing of the debt and then being unable to pay it. Whatever next?

"What if we sold some possessions? Or even livestock or horses? Surely they are worth something?" she asked.

The steward shook his head. "I'm sorry, no. The estate and all its assets are entailed, along with this London townhouse. There is nothing we can sell, apart from your dresses. Those are owned by you, and you may do with them what you please."

Kate shook her head, her outrage toward George growing by the minute. How could he leave them in such a situation? Of course, she had little doubt he thought the duke would forgive the debt. What friend would not think so since they were once very close? But not Montague, it would seem. He would not forgive anything at all.

"Well, thank you for explaining everything to me as it stands, Mr. Smith. I appreciate you discussing this matter with me on such short notice, and I will take everything you've said to me and consider it." While Kate did not know how to escape this mess, there had to be a solution.

Mr. Smith stood, gathering up his paperwork and ledgers. "I suggest you ask your brother, Lord Astoridge, for assistance. I do not wish to speak out of hand, but it was rumored that Lady Astoridge, his wife, had quite a sizable fortune upon their marriage. Should you need their help, I'm certain they would offer it to you without question."

Kate stood and walked Mr. Smith to the library door. "I'm certain they would, and I will think of that suggestion too." Not that she would ask her brother. Paris had already saved the Astoridge family from certain ruin once before. She couldn't ask her to do such a thing again.

Kate saw off Mr. Smith and headed back into her office, needing to pen a missive to the duke. He was waiting for a response and had given her until tomorrow, but nothing was left for it. She would have to explain that she did not have the money and he would have to wait a while longer.

Two or three years is not a little while, Kate...

She sat at her desk and scribbled a short, to-the-point note to His Grace. No doubt he would call early tomorrow and demand his funds. She laid down the quill and took in the room, the paintings, the furniture. Surely, no one would ever know if she sold some of the contents.

The thought of her little boy and her taking what was rightfully his by birth shamed her. No, she could not sell anything, so what could she do?

For several minutes, she debated that very question before a solution so scandalous and not to mention ruinous floated through her mind.

The duke had once asked her to promenade, which she had always thought hinted at him being romantically attracted to her.

Could he still be? Would he be open to her paying back this horrendous debt by other means? Means by which she became the payment? He was famously wealthy. Indeed, many suggested he was more affluent than the Duke of Devonshire.

The idea did not horrify her as much as it should. The duke was a powerful, not to mention utterly delectable gentleman who turned every woman's gaze his way whenever he entered a room.

Who would not want to work off debt under such a

specimen? The only question was, would he be willing to allow her to?

———

Wolfe arrived at Lady Brassel's townhouse at the precise time he was allotted per her missive and not a minute before. He handed his top hat and gloves to the elderly butler and followed the stooping fellow into the library.

He schooled his features to an expression of indifference the moment he caught sight of Lady Brassel. Today, she wore an azure morning dress made of muslin that made her dark-blue eyes shine brighter than he'd ever seen them before.

She gestured to the seat in front of the desk. "Good morning, Your Grace. Please do sit down." She sat. He did the same, hoping that a banknote would be ready so he could depart and put this component of his life behind him.

The money or Lady Brassel behind you?

Wolfe ground his teeth, ignoring the voice in his head. "Good morning, Lady Brassel. I must say I'm pleased by your summons. I hope that means good news for me and my coffers."

Her face paled, and annoyance flitted through him. She did not have the money. The question was, what was she going to do about the problem?

"As promised, I had a meeting yesterday with our steward, and I'm sorry to inform you that I cannot raise one thousand pounds at present. I questioned if I could sell some property, which I was informed I could not. I also considered asking my brother and his wife for assistance, but I decided against this. I'm sorry to disappoint you, but I cannot pay the debt."

Wolfe took a calming breath and hoped her ladyship did also after that tirade of words—that would not end as he would have liked—spilled out of her. He watched and noted the glistening of sweat on her upper lip, the muscle that worked in her jaw.

He did not like to pressure anyone, especially a woman, but nor could he be taken for a fool. Brassel lost the money fair and square, and now someone had to pay him back.

"And so you are asking me to forgive the debt or have some other idea on how to resolve this issue."

She licked her lips before clamping the bottom one between her teeth. He swallowed, the action spiking heat where no heat ought to be spiking right at this moment.

But there was no denying his attraction to the woman before him. Before Brassel, he had coveted Miss Kate Astoridge himself. That Brassel won her was due to his friendship with Brassel and not wishing a woman to come between them. Not that his life up to now had not been most enjoyable, shamefully so, but he had always wondered "what if" when it came to Lady Brassel.

"I know you will not forgive the debt, but will you give me more time?"

"No, there is no time, as I said. I'm leaving London soon." He sat back in the chair and crossed his arms, losing patience. Brassel, had he not already been dead, would be after he got his hands on the beggar who squandered more money than he made.

Damn fool...

"Very well," she said, linking her hands on the desk before him and leveling a steely gaze his way. "You leave me with no other option than to offer another way to pay the debt."

"Another way?" Curiosity had him leaning forward before he righted himself and sat back. "Do tell me your idea. I'm all ears," he drawled.

"Well, as to that, Your Grace. And please do not laugh, jest, or censure me for what I'm about to say. I have thought over the proposition, and to keep my son's inheritance intact and the estate safe, this is my suggestion. You may approve or disapprove, but please do so with respect."

"Very well." Wolfe steeled himself for whatever it was she was about to say. Something told him he'd like what she offered. Somewhere deep down in the dark recesses of his soul, the wolf in him growled in expectation. "Tell me your proposal."

"I propose I become your mistress secretly until the debt is paid."

Everything in Wolfe stilled, and he basked in the idea of having her under him for a moment before reality struck him back to sense. "Absolutely not, Lady Brassel. You will never be my mistress."

THREE

Wolfe had never heard of anything so outlandish in his life. Should he take up Lady Brassel on her proposition, he would be making her his whore, not just a mistress. Did she even understand that fall from grace in her quest to keep her son's inheritance safe?

"Why not, Your Grace? This is the only option available. I cannot pay you the sum required, but I'm willing to...do other things that may be to your liking. Your reputation..."

"I know I have a reputation, madam," he snapped, halting her words and not wanting to hear another about who and what he was. The Wild Wolfe of London was very well, but that did not make him into whatever it was that Lady Brassel was trying to get him to agree to. He could not bed a woman in payment for funds owed. He knew he had minimal standards when it came to fucking, but this was entirely crossing a line.

"I'm a widow now, and my son is my priority. I do this willingly so long as we're discreet and no one ever finds out what went on between us, not even my family. I would be ruined, and so too would my son should we ever be caught."

Wolfe studied her and noted the determination that burned in her eyes. "My sexual appetite does not have the title of wild in it for nothing, my lady. Should I agree, and I'm not in any way saying that I will, but if I should, you must know that I could ask anything of you and wherever that fancy took me. A ball, a park, carriage, wherever it may be, if I want you, I will have you." He leaned back in his chair, hoping his relaxed stance after stating such a scandalous demand would scare her off, but if anything, she only followed his action, leaning back in her chair and nodding in agreement.

"I'm willing to do whatever you wish and where you wish to do it, so long as you're not cruel or demeaning."

"I am never either of those things." Wolfe fought not to be insulted by her words and failed. Was that what she thought of him? Some rutting, angry animal who took what he wanted without care for the woman beneath him?

Damn...

"Then I do not see why we cannot agree to these terms. All that is left to discuss is how long you would expect me to be your lover. A month, I thought, would suffice."

Wolfe scoffed. Was she serious in her timeline? "I think not, my lady. A month, and we're only just getting started. If I agree, you shall be my mistress for the remainder of the Season. I shall put off my leaving for Scotland and enjoy bedding you until I travel north."

A rosy hue kissed her cheeks, and her swallow was almost audible. Wolfe inwardly chuckled, enjoying her embarrassment. And so she should be ashamed after asking him to engage in such an agreement. A mistress indeed.

"But that's three months. Surely, that is a little lengthy for such a sum owed."

He shrugged, not caring the least about what she thought on the matter. If he were not getting a thousand pounds, not that he needed it in truth, he would get his money's worth with her. "Those are my terms. You can agree to them, or I shall consult my lawyer on how I can recoup the funds owed to me by your husband in another way. You came up with this absurd idea. The choice is yours." Wolfe knew he was unyielding and cold but could not help himself. The thought of bedding Lady Brassel had long been a desire that had haunted him for years. He did not like losing, and that Brassel had begged him to stand aside still irked.

Even so, he did not think when it came to actually doing the deed that she would go through with it. She would relent, run screaming, and possibly faint when she saw the size of his cock. It would not be the first time a woman had done so.

"Very well, until the end of the Season. You may come here, or I shall travel to you, but it must be without notice. That you must promise me," she stated.

He nodded, and somewhere through their conversation, he seemed to have agreed to this outrageous plan. Still, he did not want to let her know that just yet. He would let her stew on the troubles that faced her a little longer and come back next week with his response.

"I shall return and let you know what I have decided. There is much to take into account. Having sex with you, while I'm sure it will be enjoyable, I do wonder if it'll satisfy my needs. You are a titled lady, and they're known to be like bedding sacks of potatoes that do little but roll around. I will give you a week to think about this. When I take a woman to bed, know that I enjoy the act of giving pleasure as well as receiving it." He purposefully looked at her mouth. She bit her lip yet again, and fire shot to his groin. "Your mouth, in particular, will be needed to lower the deficit."

Her pretty lips opened with a gasp, and he stood, knowing this conversation had to end now, before he bent her over the desk and took his first payment.

"Good day to you, Lady Brassel. I will be in touch soon."

K ate's body burned with an unknown feeling she had never experienced. The way the duke spoke, what he had suggested and hinted at, especially when it came to her mouth...surely that was impossible. What she imagined could not be done. He would not expect her to...

She stood, walked to the sideboard where George kept his whisky, and poured herself a large glass. Sipping it, she strolled to the window and watched the Duke of Montague mount his horse. The man certainly drew the eye, and several ladies on the street stopped to gape and enjoy seeing him on the back of his charge.

And why would they not? His muscular legs and broad shoulders hinted at a man whose body beneath was as hard as his manners.

He flicked her stable lad a coin and walked his horse on, his attention forward, never looking back to see if she was watching, but something told her he knew she was.

She doubted there was much that got past him.

She sat on the window sill, debating her choice and what she had offered. Could she really have sex with the duke and not hate herself forever for stooping so low?

It was not as if she were being unfaithful to Brassel. He

was gone now, and she had been a good wife and friend to him. Him, not so much in return after leaving them with such a hefty price to pay.

But she would not allow anything to jeopardize her son's future. Before her brother had married Paris, they had been in financial trouble, and she did not like the idea of history repeating itself.

No, she would sleep with the duke, which would be enjoyable if the rumors were true and not the opposite. He said himself he would give pleasure as well as take his own, whatever that meant. Was he suggesting sex to be satisfying? She had never known it to be...

But her mouth?

Kate downed the last of the whisky and set it aside. Her attention moved to the hundreds of books in the library, and she stood. "Surely there must be books here about the sexual conduct between husbands and wives."

She walked the room for several minutes, searching for books on anatomy, sexual intercourse, anything that may help her understand, be prepared, and not so potato-like as he stated.

Whatever that meant...

A book titled *The Natural and Excellent Amours of Lord Scandal* caught her attention, and she opened it. Kate gaped at the first image sketched and described and where one could use such a position. She turned the book one way and the next, trying to figure out how that would be possible between a couple.

Indeed, it was not.

Even so, the more she flicked through the pages, the more she understood that perhaps she had bitten off far more than she should have. How was she to please the Wild Wolfe of London when, in truth, he was right?

Kate stood in the middle of the room, the book falling to her side. Whatever had she done? She could never live up to his expectations.

Dear Lord, she was a potato and doomed to displease him in bed.

FOUR

True to his word, the duke took one week and a day before he called on her again. In that time, she had debated throwing herself at her brother's mercy. Telling her sister that she was a woman of loose morals and fleeing to the Americas where she would not have to face what she knew she must. Or merely running away so the duke could never find her again.

How could she have offered herself as a form of payment for her husband's debt, and to one of London's most notorious rogues?

He would laugh at her. See her naked form and cringe.

After giving birth to her son, her body was not the same as her youthful appearance had been. Not that it was terrible in her estimation; her body now bore the marks of a mama who had birthed a son, and happily so.

But the Wild Wolfe of London, she doubted, was used to bedding such women. She clasped her stomach as nerves tumbled through her yet again.

How could she have offered such a payment? The image of her child flittered through her mind, and she knew the answer to that question. She would not let him suffer the consequences of his father's flawed money management and his inability to keep out of gaming hells.

Foolish man. Had she known of the debt, she would have forced his hand when he was alive.

"I have laid out a list of everything I expect when taking a lover. It's quite detailed, and only some things we shall do, but I like to be upfront with the mistresses I take into my bed. It stops any awkward conversations later, you understand."

The duke slid the document toward her, and she glanced at it, unsure if she wanted to read it. After everything she had seen in the book *The Natural and Excellent Amours of Lord Scandal*, to read what the duke wanted seemed too much for her sensibilities.

"You will need to read it, madam," he said, his voice brooking no argument.

Kate sighed and reluctantly picked it up. She sat back in her chair and held the paper up before her face so he could not see her reactions to the words that jumped out.

What on earth was to tip one's velvet or to ride rantipole, for that matter? Dear Lord, did he expect her to be some caterwauling woman who could do tricks for him at will?

Schooling her features, she placed the paper back onto the desk and levelled him with a direct stare. "Like I said, Your Grace. I'm willing to do as you wish, so long as the debt is paid by the end of the Season," she lied, knowing she would not be doing any of those things unless she knew what they meant. "But there is one thing I would like to add to our agreement, which I think after reading what you expect from me is only fair."

The duke steepled his fingers in his lap, his eyes

narrowing as he contemplated her words. "Very well, I'm a man who can compromise in some aspects of my life. Do tell me what you would like revised."

Kate swallowed her nerves and ignored that today, the duke wore an ebony tailcoat with a squared cut away in front and tan breeches that sat upon his form like a second skin. The tailor had perfectly cut the garment to fit his every measurement. His eyes, as sharp and flawless as his clothing, watched her like a hawk and rarely missed anything.

He was much too big for this room. His energy sucked all the air out of any space, no matter that her library was as large as her ballroom.

"I would like to amend our agreement to clarify that should anyone find out about our affair, the debt will be forgiven, and no further interactions will occur. It will be bad enough should anyone find out we're having an affair, nevertheless to continue and make everything worse for us both."

The duke remained silent, his eyes never leaving hers, and Kate fought the urge to fidget. Why did he make her so nervous? What was it about this man that put her all at sixes and sevens? She did not have this response with George, not even when they were courting.

But the duke... Well, he was another matter entirely.

"This is not an affair. Let us be clear on that, madam. Furthermore," he said in a tone that sounded far less pleased than it had a minute ago. Was he insulted by her request? That she did not know, but nor could she continue with this arrangement should scandal break out. She did not want to lose her reputation entirely.

"I want to remind you that this is your suggestion, not mine. Yes, I'm here, and being here shows my agreement with your plan, but this is not an affair. You'll be my lover if you prefer the word to mistress. I shall only engage with a mistress after our agreement ends. But there is no emotion, no feelings between us. Please understand that before we start. If you agree to do so, I'm happy with that clause being included in our verbal agreement."

"Very well, Your Grace, then yes, I'm happy with our terms, and I'm willing to start whenever you wish."

Now that Wolfe had heard Lady Brassel state she was willing and ready, the thought of doing anything with the woman sent a wave of panic through him.

He had stayed away a week, confident she would change her mind. Find some way in which to pay him what was due without the use of her body. And yet, sitting before her, a woman he had long admired and coveted from afar, agreeing to fuck him whenever he wished, well, that was another matter entirely.

What the hell was he supposed to do with her now?

Not that he couldn't think of a thing or two, but to do anything with her after they had discussed the matters of their agreement like two lawyers seemed wrong.

Certainly, it did not make his cock hard.

"You've only just re-entered society, so we can meet at balls and parties, but I can escort you home, or you can visit me at my residence. I'm certain there will be plenty of opportunities for us to be together."

Lady Brassel nodded, her eyes wide and watchful. He could not blame her. He wasn't known to be a cully coxcomb type of gentleman the ladies hankered for. Women loved him for another reason entirely, which Lady Brassel would relish when the time came.

Just as he certainly would.

"Under the cover of darkness, too, if you please."

The thought of her only wanting to have sex with him at night amused him, and he laughed. "Are you telling me you never had sex with Lord Brassel during the day? Did you not like being naked before his lordship when he could see you as clearly as you are now?"

Had he not been watching her, he would have missed her small flinch at his words. He narrowed his eyes, wondering if he was right in that estimation.

"I merely do not wish for anyone to see us. That is my only concern, and while we're discussing this agreement further, there is no need to call me Lady Brassel. Kate will do just fine. We have known each other for several years, and hearing you say my married name makes me feel as though I'm being disloyal."

Wolfe thought about what she was asking, debating whether that would be a wise idea. He did not think so. Calling her Kate made what they were doing feel far more intimate than he liked.

Not to mention that he'd once craved to hear her give him leave to call her by her given name.

"Lord Brassel is gone...*Kate*. No one is being unfaithful, other than his lordship who died and did not pay his dues to his faithful friend."

She sighed, clearly annoyed at him, but he did not care. That was the truth; nothing, no sighs or looks of annoyance, would change that fact.

"Very well then, there is just one thing left for us to do, and that is commence this agreement. What would you like me to do first, and when? I want to be prepared before you call. I do not like spontaneity."

Wolfe cleared his throat and stood, feeling as though fucking Kate would be a chore that even his rakehell side did not cherish. He did not like sex to be a duty. Where was the fun in that when sex was planned like an appointment? He'd never operated that way, and he certainly wouldn't start now.

He leaned on the desk, crowding her. A little part of him filled with satisfaction when she did not back down but merely stared back, determined not to show trepidation.

"I will call when I feel like fucking you, Kate, and not before and not today. All this talk of contracts and clauses has me limp in the pants," he said, smiling at her startled gasp. "But I may call through the day or night, so it is best to be always prepared."

"That is impossible," she called as he walked from the room.

"But you will be," he replied. "Because that is what we agreed."

CHAPTER
FIVE

The ball held each year in the gardens of Lord and Lady Astor's home was a crush. Everyone swarmed outside to enjoy the riverside home and the punting they included for their guests as added entertainment. The ball being a masque this year added a sense of recklessness and mystery, but even with a mask on every guest's face, he could pick out Lady Brassel anywhere.

Wolfe leaned against a tree, keeping to the shadows, and watched Lady Brassel re-enter society as a dowager countess. And what a pretty dowager she made, with several gentlemen eyeing a prize that was his to claim.

The only question was when would he do so?

The thought of taking her to his bed sent a bolt of desire to course through his blood, but it also gave him pause. He'd once coveted the woman, had wanted her for himself when he'd been young, and fell heedlessly in love every other day.

But there had always been something about Lady Brassel that he'd never quite plucked from his heart. She was like a thorn stubbornly stuck under his skin.

He pushed away from the tree and strolled into the throng of guests, speaking only to those who offered words of welcome. He'd never been one for small talk and didn't think to start now.

Lady Brassel had her back to him as he came up behind her. Her sister's eyes widened as she watched his every move and only fleetingly smiled when he joined them.

"Good evening, Your Grace. We hope you're enjoying the masque as much as everyone else here this evening," Lady Orford said with an air of cautiousness, her attention snapping to her sister before returning to him.

Had Lady Brassel confided any of their agreement to her sister? He couldn't help but think yes from Lady Orford's cool demeanor. But then Kate had said she wanted utter secrecy, so maybe Lady Orford's wariness of him stemmed from his reputation...and she would be right.

"I'm finding it well enough, thank you, Lady Orford. But I come bearing a message. Lord Orford would like to speak to you. He's near the Thames gate, I believe."

"Oh, does he? I shall go directly."

Before Lady Brassel could stop her sister from leaving her alone with him, he clasped her hand and placed it on his arm, walking them toward the outdoor ballroom. "A dance, Lady Brassel."

"Well, considering you're leading me there like a truffled-up cow, I seem to have little choice in the matter."

His lips quirked, and he could not disagree. "I was your late husband's friend. There is nothing untoward or strange about us talking or dancing. You're out of mourning, and I want to get a feel for what shall be mine soon enough."

She met his eyes and glared. "You're repulsive. And I do not like you using the term mine. It is untrue and not what we agreed."

He did laugh then and pulled her against him closer than he ought as he waited for the waltz to begin. "And what is to occur is entirely your doing. You know you may still pay me, and nothing will come to pass. You will not warm my bed, and I shall not ruin all your memories of Brassel and his rutting with my fucking that you will surely enjoy more."

"While I'm certain you do not mean to be crude or disrespectful to the dead, I'll have you know that George was a sweet, careful husband and never spoke to me in such a coarse, garish manner."

"And yet again, this was your idea, so who really is the most vulgar here? Some would say you were." He inwardly crowed at besting her on that point, but also, a part of him wondered why he baited her so.

He had kept away from this polite society as much as he could during the years since they had first met, but he was still one of them. He was not out of place here, even if she wished he were so. He had nothing against Lady Brassel directly. She was merely a means by which to be paid.

Maybe just being near Lady Brassel makes you ill at ease.

Willing to ponder that quandary another day, he said, "At least pretend that you're enjoying the waltz." He spun her around the ballroom floor. "People will talk if they think a falling out between us has occurred."

"I may have devised this preposterous idea, but you agreed and will not forgive the debt. What other options do I have than to do everything that you say? One may even express that you're allowing this agreement to continue and not forgive the debt because deep down in your dark soul, you want us to be lovers."

He inwardly stilled at hearing her call them lovers. In truth, he could not wait to fuck her. To have her writhe

26

beneath him, for him to taste her sweet lips, and the ones on her mouth too.

"I'm more than willing to sweep you off this dancefloor and have you screaming my name within a few minutes in the shadowed gardens if you'd like."

Her eyes widened, and she scoffed, but even with her black mask covering her eyes, he could see the blush that stole across her cheeks. "You do think highly of yourself. A few minutes and I'm supposed to feel pleasure. Do be serious."

Was she challenging him? He wrenched her close, far too familiar than was proper, but others enjoying the dance failed to notice what was happening nearby.

"Just say the word, Kate, and I shall prove I can. I like nothing more than a challenge, and a widowed dowager who I doubt has ever felt pleasure in her life would not take long to gasp my name."

K ate did not know how she had come to get herself into this pickle and in the middle of a masque ball, but here she was. Baiting one of London's most notorious men, who she did not doubt for a second could do what he threatened.

And that was the rub. Was it really a threat? Or something she had inwardly craved for so long? She had seen it on her sister's face. The secret smiles between Anwen and her husband when they thought no one was watching. The dreamy eyes that Anwen often had in the morning that took forever to focus on the tasks at hand.

Was this what the Wild Wolfe of London was threatening her with?

She had lost George over a year ago now, a long time to

be alone. Her son was being schooled at home at their country estate while she was in London; in truth, she was lonely.

Even so, she could not scuttle off into the bushes and allow him to have his way with her. And what would that entail anyway?

She wished she were not so naïve on the matter of sex.

"I gasped George's name and often," she lied. "You do not know what you speak of."

A muscle worked in his jaw, and he looked displeased, no longer teasing as he had a moment before. "There is something about you saying those words I cannot believe. You forget that I knew George, that I knew him before you rushed off and married him. You lie when you say you called out his name during the height of release. I'm certain of it."

Kate swallowed and schooled her features. What release did he speak of? She wished she had spoken more in-depth about married life with Anwen. She was sure her sister knew what the duke meant.

Deciding to ignore the last of his words, she chose the safest option, which was to change the subject entirely. "What do you mean to rush off and marry George? I never did anything of the kind. He courted me for the duration of the 1815 Season, and anyway, what does it matter to you if I did rush into marriage or not? It was not as if you were hoping to marry me instead."

The duke turned his attention to those around them and did not meet her eye for several turns of the dance. "You, like so many of your ilk, always rush into marriage with men as long as your position and security are ensured. You maybe should have schooled your enthusiasm regarding the match. You may then know what I'm talking about when it comes to enjoying sex with a man."

"I beg your pardon. I do know what you mean," she spat before she could think better of her words.

The smug turn of his delectable, kissable lips made her want to scratch his eyes out or demand he show her what he was so good at and no one else, in his opinion.

His hand moved on her back, dipping low on her gown to sit scandalously close to her derrière. "Do not worry, Lady Brassel. Now that we've formed an agreement, you will know soon enough what it's like to be satisfied in bed. So much so that I would lay a wager right now that you'll be begging me to fuck you again."

She would take that bet, the cur. "A wager worth a thousand pounds?" she asked.

He chuckled. "Oh hell no, you're not escaping my bed that easily."

CHAPTER
SIX

After the waltz, Kate managed to slip away and find the retiring room indoors. She sat on one of the chaise longues and fought to calm her racing heart.

Never in her life had she ever been spoken to in such a raw and unfiltered way, and never by a man. But it was not any man. It was Montague, the Wild Wolfe of London.

It did not help her equilibrium that her body came alive with every word he spoke. Her heart beat fast. Her skin prickled with awareness, and heat pooled at her core. Something about the man drew her like poor Brassel never had.

Was she a terrible person for feeling this way? While panic-inducing, the idea of taking His Grace to her bed was also an expectation that she had not thought to feel.

"There you are, Kate. I've been looking for you everywhere."

Kate looked up to see her sister enter the retiring room with a relieved smile. "Yes, I needed a break. Did you find Lord Orford? Is everything well?" she asked.

Anwen plopped down beside her, a look of annoyance on her features. "I did find Daniel, and he never asked for me, which brings me to why I sought you out here. What did Montague want with you? I saw you dancing with him after he lied to be rid of me."

He lied? Kate shushed Anwen as several young ladies bustled into the room. "Just to dance and reminisce about George."

Her sister stared at her, and Kate could feel the heat climbing up her throat. She remained quiet and hoped Anwen would drop the topic.

"I think you forget that as your *twin* sister, I know you better than anyone, and that means I also know when you're lying. The top of your ears go red, which they are doing right now, so do not think that your dancing with the duke is nothing. Now, explain Kate."

Kate inwardly sighed. She could not tell Anwen what she had agreed to. Her sister would storm from the room and, if she knew her sister at all, go right up to the duke and assault his ears verbally.

"You know that he was one of George's friends. He's merely being nice to a widow who's stepping back into society after a year. Nothing more than that, I assure you."

"Well, you both certainly cut a dashing pair on the dancefloor. And if I'm to endure the Season as promised, then at least tonight has started well. Maybe now that you're out of mourning, the duke wishes to court you and is merely seeing if you'd be open to such a friendship. Not that I'm entirely at ease with this. He is a rake, after all."

If only that were true and his interest in her was not her own shameful idea. "He is not," she said. Kate would not mind so much should she be courted or called up with flowers and gifts. It would be nice after everything that had

31

happened to her and her son, but it was not the case. The duke wanted payment, and he would get that payment with her pound of flesh.

How she regretted ever voicing such an arrangement. He was too much a man. He took up too much space, was overbearing, and was far too sharp-witted for her. His handsomeness made her catch her breath each time she looked at him.

Wolfe indeed...

"Well, I think you're wrong."

Anwen went behind a screen to relieve herself, and Kate fought to school her features. She did not want her sister to get one whiff of the understanding, and she would need to be competent to ensure that she and society never learned of it.

"I am not wrong," she said when Anwen rejoined her. "Everyone knows he has a long-standing mistress and has no interest in marriage. I think it is nice that he's being kind to me. Coming back into society is not the easiest when people look upon you with pity after losing one's spouse." It was also not easy when society did not know that one's marriage, although happy, was not a passionate love match. Brassel was kind, but he did not love her. Although she was sure he loved the idea of her being his wife more than the actual marriage itself.

"Well, I will live in hope that you find love, Kate. You deserve to be as happy as I am, and I know Brassel would want that too."

Kate stood and embraced her sister before leading her toward the door. She had sat in the retiring room long enough. Not that she would return to the ball and have to face the duke again. Oh no, she was too much a coward for that. Instead, she would return home. The evening had been taxing enough, and she wasn't sure she enjoyed how her body betrayed her every time she caught sight of Montague.

W olfe stood in the foyer of Lord and Lady Astor's home and waited for his carriage to be brought around. Light footsteps sounded behind him, and the softly spoken words from a woman who had occupied far too much of his thoughts these past days spoke at his back.

He turned and watched with satisfaction as a footman handed Lady Brassel her shawl. She turned to leave and skidded to a stop at the sight of him.

She did not expect to see him here, an obvious fact. Was the woman trying to leave the ball without saying goodbye? Without making a little partial payment toward her late husband's debt?

"Are you ready, Lady Brassel? My carriage has arrived." Without waiting for her to respond, not that he thought she would be able to, not if the silence that seemed to have taken over the countess after being caught trying to escape were any indication.

She followed him without question, clearly not wishing to make a scene, and he was grateful for it. The fewer people who noted their leaving together, the better. Not that anyone was around, other than the staff.

He helped her into the carriage and noted the tremble in her fingers. Was she truly scared of him? Perhaps he had been too coarse and cold concerning their arrangement.

But what did she expect? There were no emotions or feelings between them, and he'd never been a gentleman to whisper sweet sonnets merely to get his way with a woman. They either took him as he was or not at all.

They settled on the velvet squabs, and not wanting to make her appear any more frightened than she already did, Wolfe sat across from her. He drank in the vision of her, so beautiful tonight that he felt his breath catch the moment he had seen her.

She reached up behind her head and untied the ribbons holding her mask, revealing her pretty face. "Now that we're alone, what is it you wish to do?"

He bit back a chuckle laced with hunger that would see her fleeing for the hills. "What would you suggest? You read my list. Why don't you choose a form of payment agreeable to you."

She bit her lip, and he took a calming breath. Damn, her lips were delectable, a little pouty, and perfect for kissing, for sucking, among other things.

"I'm not sure I'm comfortable with anything, Your Grace. I think I've made a mistake."

Disappointment stabbed low in his gut, but he knew she would balk and ask for an out. It was only a matter of time, as he suspected.

"Very well. I shall have the thousand pounds by week's end."

"Fine," she seethed, punching the seat on either side of her. He watched, enthralled, as her temper got the better of her, and she moved across the carriage to sit beside him. Without a word, she clasped his face and kissed him.

Hard.

Everything inside Wolfe stilled and then blasted into a firestorm of desire and need. So much need that his cock stood to attention. The kiss at first was unfamiliar. She kissed him but did not move. She merely held her mouth against his as if she did not know what to do.

He would not have it.

Had she never been kissed properly before, either? Brassel ought to be horse-whipped for not kissing Kate as she deserved.

Wolfe pulled back and met her eyes. "Relax your mouth and open it a little for me. You'll enjoy it more. Trust me."

Her eyes wide, her body trembling, she nodded and did as he suggested. He closed his mouth over hers, teased her with his tongue, and felt the axis of his world shift.

Her lips were soft, so smooth that it was like kissing a pillow of air. She opened, and he teased her tongue with his, satisfaction spiking through him when she followed his cue.

Relaxed. Gave way to desire.

And for the very first time in his life, the Wild Wolfe of London did not feel tame...

CHAPTER
SEVEN

Kate fumbled for purchase as Montague kissed her with a vigor that left her reeling. What was happening between them? What was she doing, throwing herself at his head and kissing a man she barely knew?

Not that he was a total stranger. Brassel did speak of him often, but they rarely spoke at events and parties before her husband's death, so to be kissing him, going along with her absurd plan, was confounding, if not confusing.

But oh, how utterly delicious were his kisses. His mouth moved on hers with such an expertise that one forgot all about what was proper, wrong, and right and let themselves float into the ether of desire.

His fingers spiked into her hair, the pins scattering to the carriage floor. The wheel dipped into a hole in the road, sending her tumbling against him.

The kiss changed, morphed into something wild and wanton, hard and demanding. Kate threw herself into all that he offered. Never had she felt so alive, her body burning with unsated need.

And that was what was most frightening of all. How much she wanted from the duke after one kiss. One kiss would never be enough, not now that she had a taste of the wickedness that he offered.

He reached for her and settled her on his lap, never once breaking the kiss. Their tongues danced, tangled, and teased. Against her hip, she could feel the hardened length of his manhood, the impression much more significant than she expected.

But then, he was renowned for his prowess, his rakehell ways. Why would he not be blessed with a penis that was as overbearing as he was?

"Command me to touch you," he whispered against her lips.

It took her a moment or two to understand what he was asking. She met his eye and clasped his hand that sat on her hip. Without answering, she slid it up her abdomen, watching his eyes darken and burn with hunger.

She shivered, having never seen anyone so affected by her before. Was she truly in a carriage with Montague and allowing him to seduce her to within an inch of her life?

For she would surely die from the exquisiteness of it all.

"Touch me," she asked him, placing his hand on her breast.

Determination crossed his features before he kissed her again. Their mouths fused in a battle of wills of who could make the other lose themselves quickest.

His fingers slipped the bodice of her gown down before his thumb and forefinger teasingly pinched and rolled one nipple.

A spike of pleasure shot between her legs, and she

squeezed them tight, having never experienced anything like that before. It was as if he had touched her at her most private of places.

He broke the kiss, dipping his head to kiss his way down her neck, taking a moment to tease her earlobe and shoulder before halting at her exposed breast.

His tongue flicked out, and Kate gasped, clutching Montague, anything to stop herself from falling off his lap.

"Oh, you like that," he murmured against her skin, his warm breath sending a shiver of delight down her spine.

She nodded, bit her lip, and waited for more. But he wanted more than one taste.

"Tell me you like it," he commanded, meeting her eyes.

Kate swallowed and watched him, feeling that he was on the verge of stopping if she did not do as he said.

"I love it," she admitted, biting down the shadow of shame that settled over her at her admission.

Was it so wrong to enjoy such an interlude? Yes, she was paying back a debt, but never had she ever wanted a man as much as she wanted Montague. She was a young woman, her whole life ahead of her. There was nothing immoral about wanting an experience that may never be offered to her again.

Was there?

His mouth closed about her nipple, and she forgot her doubts and guilt. His tongue swirled as his lips kissed, his hand squeezed and taunted her breast, and all the while, sharp stabs of desire seized her cunny.

"You're very reactive," he stated. "I enjoy it too." He kept teasing her breast. He ripped her bodice down, revealing the other.

Kate arched on the squabs, the duke between her legs,

paying homage to her breasts and sending her spiraling into a world she did not know existed.

Her body burned, her hips rising of their own accord, trying to press against the duke's groin.

"You want me. I can smell your desire." He gave her what she wanted, then clasped her legs and wrenched her to lie flat on the seat. He came over her, his engorged cock teasing her mons, undulating there as he kissed and laved her nipples.

Sensation mixed with expectation left her spinning. She clutched at his jacket and murmured incoherent words that she did not know what they meant. All she knew was she did not want him to stop.

Not ever.

And certainly not yet.

"Please, Montague," she begged him.

"Wolfe. I want to hear my name on your lips." He thrust harder against her cunny at the same moment, he suckled forcefully on her nipple.

Kate stilled as her body did something magical and new. Her core thrummed and convulsed with a pleasure that rocked through her.

"Wolfe!" Pleasure shook her every fiber, and she sucked in a startled breath, having never felt so free, so beautiful, or more womanly in her life.

For several moments, they lay entwined before the sound of the carriage on the gravel road brought her back to reality.

Wolfe sat up, corrected his cravat and jacket, and did not look at her as she scrambled to regain her seat and not appear like a woman who had just experienced a life-shattering, delightful event.

She pulled her bodice up and tied the mask back on,

hoping the staff did not notice her hair was down when, before she went out, it was up.

The carriage rocked to a halt, and she wondered what the proper etiquette was when one left another person after such an interlude.

The urge to flee overtook her common sense, and she reached for the door before the footman came down the front steps of her home.

Montague clasped her arm, stopping her. "Consider a hundred pounds removed from the debt, Lady Brassel. I thank you for the enjoyable ride."

W olfe ground his teeth as shame washed over Kate's pretty flushed features before she fled down the carriage steps and into her home.

He slammed the door closed and pounded the roof, wanting to escape from her, this house, and what he had just done.

He threw himself against the squabs and swore. What the fuck was he doing? This game he was playing was by far the worst thing he had ever done.

And he'd done some shady, vulgar things in his life.

But he never thought she would continue with her plan, and now that he had tasted her, he wasn't sure he'd let her stop it if she tried.

But how could he remain a gentleman when he treated a lady with such disrespect?

It was her choice, and this evening, she did throw herself at you in the carriage. What man would not take advantage?

He cringed and ran a hand through his hair. He ought to have set her aside and demanded she forget this deal and merely pay him what was owed.

But damn his corrupt soul to hell. She tasted like an angel. Innocent and ready to plummet into his devil-may-care lifestyle.

He had come so close to gathering up her gown and thrusting his hard dick into her weeping quim. She would have loved it, too. He could see her writhing, wrapping her legs about his hips, begging for more.

"Fuck!" he exclaimed.

What was he going to do? Continue with this game before she realized what a fool she was being and halted it. Allow her to pay off her husband's debt in his bed.

His cock jumped at the thought, and he adjusted himself. He needed to fuck something. He needed to come.

The urge to order the carriage around and return to Kate's home almost overrode his common sense.

Would she admit him? Would he be able to wipe away the hurt he inflicted on her as she left?

What kind of bastard was he to treat a woman, his friend's widow, in such a way?

"To Blackhaven's gaming hell," he called to his coachman. He would lose himself instead in vice and dice this evening and forget the dark-haired angel whom he had almost tupped in the back of his carriage.

Maybe his mistress would be there, and he could release some pent-up desire on her.

He cringed, the idea not as appealing as it once was, and that in itself was a problem. He was not known to be a man of feeling, and damn Lady Brassel to hell, she would not be the first woman to make him so.

EIGHT

The following evening at Lord and Lady Lupton-Gage's ball, Kate stood with several ladies she knew through her sister-in-law. Many of them were amusing women, particularly the Duchess of Blackhaven. Kate liked her instantly and enjoyed her vibrant and entertaining character.

"These are my distant cousins," Lady Lupton-Gage explained to everyone within their set. "They're staying with me this Season, as we're sponsoring them."

"It's lovely to meet you both," Kate said. Miss Arabella and Evie Hall were from Brighton and stood wide-eyed and clearly unused to such grandeur found in a marquess's home. They replied in kind, but something told Kate they both felt out of place and nervous, which she could understand. The *ton* was not a place that was always kind to newcomers, and the upper society loved nothing more than to find fault with a debutante. She would be sure to befriend them and try to make them both feel welcome.

When the conversation turned to last evening's masque ball, Kate glanced at the guests milling about them. She had not spied Montague yet. Not that she was looking for him. Nor would she admit to anything of the kind. The man already had a big enough ego, and he did not need to know that she had wondered where he was and if he would be attending.

"We should sneak out now when everyone is distracted with last night's gossip."

The words, whispered by Miss Arabella Hall, caught Kate's attention, and she leaned closer, wanting to know where they thought to flee.

"If we're caught, Lady Lupton-Gage will stop sponsoring us, and we'll be back cleaning houses. I do not want that," Miss Evie Hall countered, a small frown marring her soft features.

Cleaning houses? Who were these young ladies Lady Lupton-Gage was sponsoring?

"But how else are we to see the Wild Wolfe of London? It is rumored he's there right now, playing dice with Lord Irving. It is said they've been there since last evening, and the stakes are high."

Kate excused herself from the ladies and strolled the outer vestiges of the ballroom. So Montague would not be here tonight and, after seeing her to her door last evening, had retired to a gambling hell?

And was still there?

She had heard of the Duke and Duchess of Blackhaven's gambling den that the duke had owned many years before meeting Miss Ashley Woodville, but had never been there.

She stood beside an open window, the cool air kissing her skin, and wondered... Could she be daring enough to visit His Grace there? See what he was up to?

She was a widow and would not need a chaperone, but

perhaps a mask would be best. She didn't want anyone to see her there.

Why are you chasing him down, Kate?

A question she would like an answer to. Was he meeting his mistress there? Women of looser morals, not that she could speak on the matter too much, not with their current agreement in place.

But they had agreed he would not sleep with his mistress until their arrangement ended. Perhaps she could catch him out on his duplicity and be rid of this absurd agreement she had offered if she traveled there.

With her mind made up, Kate departed the ball. The Lupton-Gage home was close to hers, and it took her only minutes to grab a hooded cloak and mask.

Instead of using her carriage, she had her footman hail a hackney cab and ordered the older gentleman to take her to Blackhaven's gambling hell in the East End.

He ought to stop gambling. To see a gentleman fall low and lose more than they should have was not as exciting as it had been when he was younger. Perhaps he was getting soft in his older years.

He watched Lord Irving inwardly debate his next move, but nothing would help him when it came to his decision. Wolfe had had exceptional felicity this evening with Hazard, and nothing bar a miracle would win Lord Irving his money back.

He took in the room for the first time in some hours, leaning back in his chair to stretch while the young earl made up his mind. There were more people here than he thought, and their table had gathered quite a large crowd of onlookers.

"No more for me this evening, Montague."

"Whatever you wish," Wolfe replied, knowing that was the wisest decision the young man had made all evening. He stood and strolled the room, watching, like many others, the games that were afoot. He glanced at his watch and noted the time. He supposed he was too late to attend the Lupton-Gage ball and to have his fill of Kate this evening.

Had she looked for him? Or was she pleased he had failed to show himself?

He supposed he could not even go into the offices and see Blackhaven. His friend would undoubtedly be at the Lupton-Gage ball since his wife was friends with and circulated within that sphere of ladies.

A dark-haired beauty wearing a mask caught his attention, and he watched as she pushed through the crowds of guests and gamblers toward the back rooms of the downstairs gaming hall. Rooms reserved for gentlemen who wished for a more private audience with whomever they fancied.

Something about how she walked niggled a memory at the back of his mind, and he followed. As he came near, the scent of lilies caught him unawares, and the pit of his stomach clenched.

Kate?

He reached for her, her delectable lip clenched by her teeth when she did not know what to do or where to go. "Are you lost, Kate?" he whispered, pulling her into an empty room and closing the door.

She wrenched out of his hold and crossed her arms at her chest. "Of course not. I was looking for a way out, that was all," she said, not denying who she was.

The fool.

"No, you were not. You tell lies, but that is the least of

my concerns right now," he said, snicking the lock on the door before leaning against it.

"What are you doing here? This is no place for a lady. Not even Blackhaven's wife comes here anymore."

"I ah...well," she hedged. "I heard a rumor that you were here, and I, ah..."

"Thought that if you caught me cock deep in a woman's quim that our arrangement would be over?" He chuckled but had to give her her due for coming here herself to see what was true or not. Then again, did she dislike him so much that she was desperate to escape his clutches?

She sighed, shaking her head. "Do you have to be so crude? But yes, I suppose that was what I was thinking, and can you blame me? You do have a reputation."

"Oh yes, my reputation. But I promised you I would be faithful to you for the duration of the Season, and I will not go back on my word. But," he paused, closing the distance between them, "now that you are here, we'll use the opportunity."

"I will not sleep with you here." She backed away until she bumped into the wall.

"I do not want to tup you here, but this room does allow us to have a little fun. If you're willing to be audacious and not such a prude."

"I am not a prude." She frowned, and he could not help but admire how appealing she was when displeased.

"Turn around, Kate. We're in the peephole room, and if the sounds coming through the wall are any indication, a couple are enjoying each other just a few feet away."

"I will not look through a peephole."

"Really? Why not? They're quite amusing." He moved the painting that hid the hole and set it on the floor before looking through it himself. "Ah, Lord Amis. He's often here.

Uses this place to meet his mistress after his wife found out about the house he kept for the woman at St. John's Wood, but could not keep the bailiffs from the door."

"What? Lord Amis is here? You jest." Kate pushed him out of the way and looked herself.

He watched as her eyes flew wide, her mouth opening in a silent gasp. "I cannot believe it. I attended Lord Amis's wedding. I thought it a love match."

"It could still be a love match."

She scoffed but didn't move her attention from the couple. "Not if he has a mistress, and Lady Amis knows of it. I should think she'd be heartbroken." She paused. "Oh my."

"Oh my?" he questioned, moving to stand behind her. She did not flinch when he pressed against her back, his hands gliding around her waist. She was so soft, all womanly curves, that he ached to see her without the layers of a cloak and dress.

"Yes, he's ah... Lord Amis is kissing the woman's most private of places."

He felt her squirm and knew she enjoyed what she watched.

"Lucky bastard."

She turned, a question in her eyes. "Men do this?"

He could not halt the smirk that twisted his lips. "If a man knows how to enjoy himself and bring the lady to release, then yes, men definitely do this. And I can do it for you if you like so that you may experience it once. But only if you're brave," he taunted, knowing she would agree merely to prove him wrong.

He was not disappointed.

CHAPTER
NINE

K ate was unsure if she liked how Montague...
Wolfe, as he had asked her to call him, felt about
what he suggested.

She couldn't help but be a little curious about the act,
but could she be so brave? Could she really allow him to
kiss her *there*?

She lifted her chin, refused to cower, and appear an
untutored debutante who had never been touched by a
man. She had been married, a wife, and bedded often. She
could do this.

Couldn't she?

The Wild Wolfe of London should prove to *her* that he
was good at such things to make her call out his name, as
the woman next door did.

"What do you want me to do? There's a bed over in the
corner. Should I lie down?" she asked, hoping the heat that
kissed every part of her body was not blossoming on her face.

"No, not over there. I want you to stay right where you
are." Montague turned her about so her back was facing

him. "I want you to watch the couple in the room while I pleasure you," he whispered against her ear, sending a shiver of expectation down her spine.

She closed her eyes, reveling in the sensation and wanting more than she would ever admit to feel and relish what he promised. To repeat the wonderful sensations that overtook her person in the carriage.

He clasped her hips, shuffling her to stand a little from the wall. "Lean forward and watch the room beyond. Leave everything else to me."

Kate bit her lip and felt him kneel. He settled in front of her and lifted her gown, taking the opportunity to run his hands along her legs as he hoisted her dress.

"Hold this." With one hand, she clasped the gown at her front, exposing herself to his view.

She did not want to overthink how personal they were right now, what he was seeing. Nerves fluttered in her belly before he wrapped one large hand about her thigh and lifted it to sit atop his shoulder.

Oh dear Lord, what had she done?

"Ah, that's better, my darling. Open for me like a flower."

Was that how he viewed her? She leaned against the wall and peeped through the hole, wanting to distract herself from the soft kisses against her thighs.

He took turns, running his tongue along the inside of her leg. Her toes curled in her slippers as the warm, aching dampness settled at her core.

His hands spread her wide, and she gasped when his tongue licked along her cunny, a sensation that was as odd as it was enlightening. Her legs trembled as he kissed and teased her sensitive flesh.

"You taste divine," he growled, moving to deepen his ministrations.

Kate stood somewhat in shock, the delicious sensations much more enjoyable than when in the carriage. She peeked through the peephole and saw Lord Amis taking his lover from behind, and the sensation of Wolfe between her legs almost undid her.

Her vagina quivered, the ache painful in its taunting. Without thought, she undulated against his face, taking what he offered and seizing the moment.

Her fingers spiked into his hair, lodging him against her, any thought of embarrassment overcome by pleasure.

"How's the view?" he asked, a teasing note to his voice.

She would not show how shockingly vulnerable or wonderful he made her feel. Kate cleared her throat, determined to sound unflustered. "Lord Amis is taking the woman from behind," she said.

He growled, suckling on her core in a way that brought her wickedly close to release. "I'm going to fuck you the same, and you'll beg me not to stop."

Kate clutched at the wall, watching the other couple. Lord Amis pulled out of the woman, and Kate noted his limp manhood. Is that what happened after men found release?

The woman pushed him onto the bed and straddled his face, rolling her hips as Lord Amis did what Wolfe was doing to her now.

Dear Lord in heaven.

"Oh," she moaned, wanting the same. She wanted everything she could get from Wolfe.

"Something interests you?" he asked, his hands clutching her bottom cheeks and helping her similarly ride his face.

"Lord Amis has spent, and now they're on the bed. The woman is sitting on his ah...on his..."

"Face?"

"Yes," she gasped when Wolfe slipped one finger into her cunny, sending another cluster of sensations through her. "Oh, God, Wolfe," she moaned, undulating on him and his ministrations.

"Would you like to try it?" he asked her.

She stepped out of his hold without hesitation and with a fearlessness she did not know she possessed. "I do. I want to ride you like that."

W olfe took Kate's hand and strode over to the bed. He lay down, watching her as he positioned himself to please her best. She trembled, but persisted with his suggestion. So concupiscent that all she wanted above anything else was release.

His cock pressed hard and engorged against his breeches. Hell, he wanted to come. He'd do anything to fuck her, but he would not. She was not ready for that.

Not yet...

She straddled his chest, and he gathered her skirts, moving them out of the way. "What do I do now?" she asked, her words breathless.

"Come up here so I can kiss your sweet cunny." After the slightest hesitation, she wiggled forward. "Hold the bedhead for support. I'll be fine under your skirts, believe me."

He licked her quim, suckling on her little bead that grew each time he flicked it with his tongue. She tasted of wickedness and sweetness combined.

It did not take her long to fall into a rhythm and relax

above him. He dipped one finger into her cunny and felt her core tighten about his digit. Damn, she would feel good. He wanted to sink his cock deep into her and bask in her heat.

"Wolfe, I ah...do not stop," she begged.

Her words made his cock twitch. He suckled on her bead, fucking her with his finger before adding another.

"Oh yes," she cried out.

She undulated on his face and rode his fingers, and never had he wanted to make a woman shatter into a million pieces as he wished Kate to do so.

She mumbled incoherent words, rolled her hips and took from him, sought her release, and basked in it when it happened. Her core tightened and spasmed about his fingers, and he drank her sweet nectar as she came.

"Wolfe," she screamed, holding herself against him as she rode out her pleasure.

Fuck she was delicious.

Fuck he wanted her.

She clutched the bedhead for support before lifting from him and sitting at his side.

He sat beside her, unable to hide the satisfaction from his features after making her shatter so brilliantly.

"You do not have to look so lofty, Your Grace," she said, raising one chastising brow.

He chuckled. "It is not that. It is merely I enjoyed every minute of you riding my face. Name a time and place, and I shall do it again. Do not doubt it."

She smiled; it was the first time he had seen her appear more benevolent toward him. Her attention moved over his body to his raging hard-on in his pants that stood out like a beacon of light in a dark sea.

"You did not find pleasure like I did?" she asked. He stilled when her hand moved over his falls and cupped his cock. "You're still hard. I never noticed with Brassel how he appeared after we were intimate. He always went back to his room and rarely spoke. But tonight, I noticed with Lord Amis he was limp, but you are not."

"I'm rarely limp. Have you not heard the rumors?" he teased.

"I have, but I do not believe that for a moment." She kneeled at his side and quickly disposed of the buttons holding his falls closed.

His cock sprung free, and she clasped him about his rod and stroked. "Lord Amis did this too. Do you like it?" she asked, rolling her thumb across the purple head of his cock.

He'd like it more if she placed her sweet lips over his manhood. "You're going to make me come, Kate. I'm already far too close."

"I want you to come. If you feel how I did, but moments ago, I think that is only fair." She tightened her grip, and he groaned, lying back and watching as she stroked his dick.

His release came quickly, his seed pulsating over his chest. She watched, fascinated, and the sight of her inquisitiveness, her enjoyment of sexual pleasure, had him growing hard again.

"How utterly marvellous." She reached out and dipped a finger into his come. Her eyes met his as she brought it to her mouth and tasted his seed.

It was Wolfe's turn to gape. It was another first in his life, but something told him it would not be his last when it came to Kate.

CHAPTER
TEN

Salty was what came to mind when she first tasted Wolfe's seed. It was not unpleasant, but certainly an odd taste that she would have to investigate further.

He watched her, his eyes darkening with a hunger that appeared wild and untamed. "I have never seen," he growled, "a woman ever do such a thing. You are quite the rare lady, Kate."

She appreciated that he thought her so and moved to lean against the wall as he stood and cleaned himself using cloths and a water bowl in the room.

She drank in the sight of him as he cleaned himself. He was such a tall, muscular man, his broad shoulders drew her eye, and she wondered when she would see him in his naked form. The idea held more merit each time she was around him, each time they were alone.

"I will take you home, or did you bring a carriage?" he asked, his tone once more businesslike and controlled.

She much preferred it when he was not so tame. Only then did she gain glimpses into the Montague she had met during her first Season. She slid off the bed and joined him at the basin, washing her hands. Inspecting her gown, she ensured it was all as it should be, including her hair, before pulling the hood over it. She spotted the mask near the side of the bed and fetched it, tying it back in place before waiting for Montague.

He buttoned his waistcoat closed and straightened his cravat. "I think we're both ready. Let us go."

She followed him to the door, he opened it, and Lord Perkins stood before them. "Montague, you devil. I wondered when whoever was in the room would be done. Have plans for it myself, you see."

"It's all yours," Montague said in a bored tone. He reached behind, took Kate's hand, and pulled her away from his lordship, another gentleman she knew and had danced with at many *ton* events.

Did all the gentlemen in London act this way? Did they all cheat on their wives? To know so many here left a hollow feeling inside. She kept her head down as they worked their way through the gambling hall and the many guests still enjoying their night of vice.

They exited the building and did not have to wait long for the ducal carriage to pull up before them, its golden family crest shining in the moonlight.

Montague helped her ascend, and she settled herself on the squabs, the memory of their last carriage ride making her stomach flutter.

The duke entered on her heels, slamming the door closed and calling out their direction. The carriage lurched forward, and for several blocks, he did not speak or look at her. Had she done something inappropriate? Was he displeased with her?

"You're angry I tried to catch you out at the hell, are you not? Or do you normally give the women you are intimate with the silent treatment after you've found your pleasure?"

A muscle worked in his jaw, and with a slowness that bordered on glacier speed, he turned and met her eye. "I enjoy sex, and when you're ready, fucking you will be most satisfying, I have little doubt. But it would be best if you did not think there is anything more between us than that. We have a deal, and women are more the emotional creatures, and I do not want you to think you'll be the future Duchess Montague or that I'll profess my undying love to you, for I will not. Marriage is not my forte."

Kate cleared the lump in her throat that choked her silent for a moment. "Do you think yourself so alluring that I shall fall at your feet at the end of our agreement and beg you to love me? I'm a countess with a child, an heir. I need never marry again, and should you not have gambled with my husband, I would not be in this situation now."

"Your husband's gambling debt is not my fault, Lady Brassel. Do try and keep up."

She glared at him then. How dare he be so rude and cold. "While it may not be your fault, it is clear that many of your supposed friends knew he had a problem keeping from any such vices, yet you allowed him to lose one thousand pounds. In my estimation, you are not much of a friend at all. Secondly, I have no romantic interest in you, Your Grace. You should be so lucky if I did."

His eyes widened, and one skeptical brow rose. "Then we're in agreement, and any intimacy between us will remain in the bedroom and not when we're in each other's company such as we are now."

"Of course, but that does not mean you must be cold and distant. You speaking to me warmly will not make me think you've fallen in love with me, Your Grace. And if you do believe it would, you think too highly of yourself." She crossed her arms and looked out the window. How she wanted to tell him off, rail at him for being such an ass. How could he think she would fall in love with him because he spoke to her with respect? The man was a Neanderthal.

"You would not be the first woman to do so, and I merely want to be clear what is happening between us."

"Oh, I'm more than aware of what is happening between us, Your Grace. I never was not."

W olfe ground his teeth and tamped down the urge to sit beside Kate, pull her into his arms, and ask her to forgive him. He did not want to be cruel or cold, but after what happened tonight between them, he no longer trusted himself that he would not want more from her.

He was obviously addled in the mind and should never have agreed to give up his mistress. The lack of sexual intercourse had made him unlike his usual self, bestowing odd sentiments he had not felt in years.

There was only one other time he had felt all lost and unsure of himself, and that was when he had asked Kate to promenade with him at Hyde Park. He was certain she would have said no. There were many gentlemen interested in courting her, and she was rarely alone at balls and parties. But she had said yes, and the excitement, the expectation that had elevated his mood for days before their promenade, was something he had never felt again since.

Until tonight.

She had been wicked, met his taunts and dares, and did not shy away from him. She was not scared of him or what he offered. Nor was she afraid to call out his ungentlemanly conduct when she saw fit.

In essence, Lady Kate Brassel was perfect.

For him...

Thankfully, right at that moment, the carriage rolled to a halt before her door, but before he could open it, she had beat him to it, swinging it wide and jumping down without the use of the steps.

"I think it is best that we have a few days apart, Your Grace. You've displeased me, and right at this moment, I do not like you at all." She slammed the door closed in his face, severing his ability to argue that point.

He watched her storm up the stairs and into her house, the shattering slam of that door assaulting his ears.

Wolfe banged on the roof and called for home. The woman would be the death of him. Maybe he should not have played with her and just forgiven the debt.

She did suggest it...

True, but did that make his actions worthy of a gentleman? They did not, and he ought to be ashamed of himself.

He thought back over the night, how he had pulled away. A gesture he often applied with all his lovers, and up until tonight, it had not bothered him that he was cold and aloof.

But seeing the disappointment, the hurt, and puzzlement in Kate's pretty features, not understanding why he was the way he was, left a hollowness inside his chest that he did not appreciate.

She did not know that he had stepped aside for Brassel. That he had wanted her for himself and each year of their marriage, having to stand aside, watch Brassel touch her, make love to her, had slowly eaten away at his politeness.

You're bitter.

He supposed that was true, and he blamed Kate for a situation that was not of her doing. It was his fault he did not fight for her, tell Brassel to bugger off. He should have fought for her hand instead of giving way.

Not that he could tell Kate any of this. That would place him in her power, and he'd be damned if he would ever allow that.

It was bad enough that should she snap her fingers and say the word, something told him he'd run to her beck and call, and the Wild Wolfe of London would finally be slayed.

CHAPTER
ELEVEN

Two nights after their last rendezvous, Kate spied Montague dancing with one of the Season's favourites, Miss Winnet Suddon. A pretty heiress from Cumbria whose father doted on her and was reportedly leaving her with everything not entailed to her elder brother.

Kate schooled her features and fought not to give way to the churning annoyance that ate at her innards. Although she could not name what was happening between them, something told her it was pushing the boundaries of their agreement.

At least, after leaving him the other night, she could not help but feel he was pushing her away. Not allowing her to get to know him, no matter how intimate they were.

Was he so against marriage that he could not even be friends with a woman? That the fear she would grow feelings for him outweighed being courteous and polite?

Montague and Miss Suddon waltzed past where Kate stood, drinking a glass of ratafia. He did not look nor acknowledge her at all. She narrowed her eyes, ignoring the warning voice that he slighted her to put her back in her place.

That place being his bed as his whore.

How had she fallen so low?

Brassel, that was why. Never before did she seethe against her husband, but she did right at this moment. To have gambled so recklessly, placing their livelihoods at risk. Put her under the power of the duke. How could he?

"Montague is very engaged this evening. First, Miss Caroline Gunn and now Miss Suddon, who seems to be enjoying her turn on the dancefloor with him. Anybody would think he's either trying to find a wife or attempting to prove a point. Which do you think it is, sister?"

Kate ignored her sister's probing and took another sip of her wine. "Where is Orford this evening? I saw you enter with Paris and Dom," she asked, changing the subject.

"He did not want to attend, and I shall not be long out, but I wanted to see you. I feel like it has been forever since we've had a moment alone."

"I saw you at the Lupton-Gage ball the other evening, Anwen." Kate reached out and clasped her sister's hand. "There is nothing wrong if you're concerned about me. I'm doing better than expected now that I'm back in society."

"Well, I was hoping that Montague would prove you wrong and seek you out as he did at the Astor ball, but it would seem his interests lie elsewhere."

At her sister's nod toward the ballroom floor, Kate watched as the duke led Miss Suddon to the side of the room where a footman stood with glasses of champagne. He handed the debutante a drink, and even from here, Kate was confident she could see his calculation on whether she would make a good prospect as a future lover.

The man was truly heinous.

Well, that wasn't entirely true. He was also appetizing, and she could understand the starry-eyed gaze Miss Suddon had set on her features. Undoubtedly, the duke knew how to toy and say pretty words to anyone he deemed worthy.

But why play the doting fool in front of her? Why now, when he had never accomplished it before? What was he trying to prove?

The pit of her stomach clenched, and she knew the answer to her question.

He was driving her away, ensuring she was situated in the box he had set out for her, but it was not working. She rattled him. His coldness the other night was proof of that.

He was propelling her away because she threatened him.

Was that fear borne out of emotion? Did she make him feel something for the first time in his life? Did he not welcome or appreciate it?

She could certainly use that to her advantage. If she continued to make him want things from her that he'd never desired from anyone else, it would only be a matter of time before he fled for the Highlands, and she would no longer have to do anything to pay off the duke.

The thought left a hollowness within her that she pushed aside. She did not want to be his lover.

No matter how wonderful and fulfilled he left her, he gave no promises, and the risks were all hers.

"What are you smiling at, sister? You appear most pleased with yourself," Anwen stated.

Kate chuckled. If only Anwen knew, and one day, maybe she would tell her sister this sorry story. But how could she not be pleased that she could possibly defeat Montague at his own game? Give her the upper hand for the first time in this game they played. Now, she merely needed to learn how to use her deductions to her advantage.

Wolfe listened as Miss Suddon drolled on relentlessly regarding her siblings, who were not old enough for a Season and still resided at home in the country.

Supposing he did not know before this evening that her home was comprised of forty-six rooms, a stable yard that could house sixteen horses and two carriages. A large ballroom with a capacity that exceeded the one in which they now stood, two wolfhounds, and five cats named Puss, Felix, Oscar, Nemesis, and Fox, well, he certainly did now.

The longer he stood at Miss Suddon's side, a debutante he had explicitly selected to irritate Lady Brassel, the more intolerable it became.

Not to mention Miss Suddon, who at every opportunity bestowed on him her many accomplishments, the most important of all, how significant her dowry was.

Not that he needed her money, and he did not particularly enjoy the notion that people may believe he was looking for a rich wife. He wasn't looking for any wife. He merely needed to rid himself of the lingering sensations that plagued him after dropping Lady Brassel off at her door.

Name them for what they are, Wofle.

Feelings.

He ground his teeth and watched as the woman of his every ire stood talking to her sister, both of their features almost identical, and yet, he could pick Kate out even at this distance.

Her nose was a little straighter than Lady Orford's, and

her hair was just a shade darker. Still, both women were striking, but Kate was the only one who ever turned his head.

Damn the chit.

He had hoped she would see him with the women he had courted this evening, whispered pretty words, and laughed when required, and yet, not once had Kate appeared the least interested in anything he did.

Maybe he worried about her catching feelings for him more than he ought.

Maybe you ought to worry about your own.

He sighed and stilled when he realized he'd done so aloud.

He looked down at Miss Suddon and could see the rosy hue kissing her cheeks that had not been there a moment before.

"Apologies, Miss Suddon. My exclamation just then was unrelated to our conversation." At least that was true, but her pursed lips told him she did not believe his words.

"If you'll excuse me, Your Grace. Lord Irving is on my dance card and I must bid you a good evening."

He bowed and let her go, hoping she was not too offended. He shook his head. What was he even doing dancing and talking to women whom he had not one ounce of interest in?

The blasted Lady Brassel had his world in a spin, and he did not appreciate the dizziness of it all.

He finished his champagne and started toward his vexation, his lover, ready to face her and perhaps enjoy a little more payment against her debt.

That is what he needed to remind himself. She owed him and had agreed to be his lover. He would not allow her to trick him into feeling sentiments that would entangle him like so many other gentlemen of the *ton* found themselves being.

He did not want her as a wife. Hell, he did not want any commitments.

"Lady Orford, Lady Brassel, good evening to you both." He bowed and pasted on a small smile, his ploy to act the gentleman never hard for a rake like himself.

"Your Grace," Lady Orford said. "You seem quite the popular gentleman this evening. Does this mean you'll finally ask a fortunate young lady to be your duchess before the Season is out?"

He cleared his throat, having not expected such a forward question, but at Kate's amused smirk, he decided to brush that smirk off her pretty face and respond just as honestly as Lady Orford had asked.

"No, not at all. Why marry a lady when I can have everything they offer without the commitment?"

Lady Orford's mouth gaped, and Kate glared at him. She wrapped her arm around his and turned to her sister. "If you'll excuse me, Anwen. The duke promised me some refreshments, and I missed supper."

Without a by your leave, Kate dragged him away from her stupefied sister, but instead of heading toward the supper room, she pulled him into a room positioned just off the ballroom.

He glanced around. Were they in a closet?

"Well, I've never fucked in a cleaning room, but there is always a first time," he said before the sting of her hand across his cheek brought him up short.

She slapped him?

He gaped at her, sure she had not, but her shocked countenance told him she certainly had.

65

CHAPTER
TWELVE

"You struck me?"

Kate raised her chin, determined not to flee the indignant and overbearing duke. Her palm stung, and she clasped her hands in her front of her to stop her from hitting some sense into him again. "Yes, I did, and I'll do it again should you speak in such a loathsome way. How could you say that to me and think that was appropriate? For all of our agreement, I'm not some doxy who's used to hearing words such as you said."

"Fucking you mean?" he stated, his mouth pulled into a displeased line.

"You're impossible. What is wrong with you that you think you can treat me like this? I know Brassel owed you money, and I'm doing all I can to pay that debt back, and I would with monetary means if I could do so, but I cannot. So if you want this to continue, I suggest you mind your manners in public."

He scoffed and rubbed a hand over his jaw. A pang of regret ran through her at his action. Had she hit him too hard? Certainly, her palm still pricked. She inwardly cringed. Maybe she ought to apologize...

At the thought, she drew herself up and halted such musings. He had not apologized, nor did he seem the least likely to.

"Like your sister minded her manners when asking who I was looking to marry? Just because she's a woman does not make her prying any less offensive or intrusive as my words when we're alone such as we are."

"Anwen does not mean it like that, and she would not wish for you to think of her that way. You are being too sensitive."

The duke's eyes widened before he threw his head back and laughed. "I'm being sensitive. You mean you're being sensitive. You knew who and what I was before we started *fucking*...do not act all offended now, my lady. It's a little late for that."

Kate sighed. Had he repeated the word to her face? "I'm returning to the ball. I have no wish to even look upon you this evening. You are clearly out of good spirits."

She stepped toward the door, and his long arms wrapped around her stomach and wrenched her backward. She stumbled into him, her bottom hitting the tops of his legs. His hands held her waist, keeping her snugly against his chest.

"You could always put me in good spirits, my lady. For all your disapproval, we are quite alone."

"We cannot do anything in here. We're but steps from the ball, and should anyone hear or see us, we'll be caught. And I'm sorry if this offends you, Your Grace, but I do not wish to be your wife any more than you wish to be my husband. Maybe you should look to the other young ladies who have gained your interest this evening. You were more than enjoying their time. You do not need to maintain mine."

"Oh ho ho, is that the way of it then? You're jealous, and were so much so that the moment we were alone, you thought to hit me. Tell me, Lady Brassel, was it because I have not waltzed with you this evening? Or partaken in a glass of champagne? That was not part of our deal. I do not remember I had to appear to be courting you to get you in my bed."

Kate grabbed one of his fingers and bent it backward until he yelped and let her go. She turned and pushed him in the chest, sending him flailing backward. "You think you're so handsome and desired, do you not? There isn't a woman in England who does not want to bed the Wild Wolfe of London, but maybe I should start a rumor. Tell everyone that I've heard you're a bore in bed. A capon or rascal that will certainly dent that too highly thought of opinion you have of yourself."

He stared at her, his eyes alight with a fire she could not explain, nor did she truly wish to. The heat that radiated from his gaze seared her very soul, and the pit of her stomach clenched.

He looked ready to murder or take her over his knee, and she would never admit to how excited that last reflection made her feel.

Why was she so mindless when he was about? He was offensive, rude, arrogant, everything she disliked in a gentleman, and yet.

And yet...

He closed the space between them and kissed her, and damn Kate's wicked soul, she melted at the first touch of his lips. He hoisted her in his hands and set her on a nearby bench. Without thought, she helped him shuffle up her gown, exposing herself to his touch.

His fingers slipped between her folds, teasing her aching flesh. Kate gasped, the sound hushed by his searing kiss.

She fumbled with the falls of his pants, ripping them open. His hard cock slipped into her palm, the skin velvety smooth, so opposite to the steel that pumped through his manhood.

Her core ached, wept for him, and she would not deny herself.

"I want you," she admitted in the shadowy room.

He reached down and placed her legs about his hips and, with exquisite slowness, eased his way inside.

"Montague." Kate pulled him closer, needing him deeper, and he did not disappoint. "More. I want more." She did not want to beg, but if he did not give her what she wanted or craved, she would expire.

She was no virginal debutante, but a widow, a woman capable of taking him to her bed.

Even if he was an infuriating rascal.

The word perfection floated through his mind as his cock sank slowly into Kate's tight heat.

Dear Lord in heaven, he was undoubtedly thanking the gods for where he was and who he was with right at this moment. He took his time, not wanting to hurt Kate. He was not a man known for his small appendage, and if he gave her time to adjust to his size, the pleasure they could have would be worth this little delay.

She was so wet and clutched his cock with a force that made stars sparkle behind his eyes. He took a breath and forced himself to calm his racing heart. Closet or not, he wanted Kate to enjoy their first time.

He ought to be ashamed for taking her here. They could be caught, and then he did not want to think what would be expected of him after the fact. But he could not regret being with her. She was perfect.

She wiggled on the table, pursuing more, and he decided it was time. He slipped out, thrust inward, and she gasped, clutched at his shoulders, her fingers curling into his superfine coat and keeping him near.

He wasn't going anywhere. In fact, right now, he could not think of one reason why he would ever want another woman again.

Unless it was Kate.

She fit him like a glove, met his every stroke. She leaned back, resting on one hand, and watched him take her. Her eyes grew heavy with desire, and he reached up, removing her other hand from his shoulder.

"Lie flat on the table. Let me fuck you until you come harder than you ever have in your life."

Her eyes widened, but she nodded and did as he asked. Her breasts threatened to spill out of her gown, and he ripped her dress higher so he could watch his cock stretch her sweet pussy each time he took her.

He wrenched her closer to the edge of the table, held her legs wide and on his hips, and thrust into her with a rhythm that made his head spin.

His balls tightened, and his cock hardened.

She moaned his name and slapped one hand over her mouth when the pleasure became too much. He could feel her small tremors and knew she was close.

The thought of her screaming his name, heedless of

where they were, made him more determined than ever to make her shatter unlike ever before.

He licked his thumb and pressed her sweet little nubbin, rolling the engorged flesh as he fucked her. She bucked beneath him, and her core spasmed, tightened so hard he gasped.

"Wolfe," she panted, coming apart in his arms.

His cock tightened on the brink of discomfort before pleasure spilled through him. He pumped his seed into her, heedless of the outcome, his knees shaking at the powerful release.

He'd never come so hard in his life, and in a sense, tonight they were both virgins, learning, experiencing sex for the first time.

He certainly had never encountered that before, and he doubted he ever would again, unless Kate was the woman in his arms after the fact.

That in itself more troubling than the risk of being caught here and now.

THIRTEEN

K ate slipped back into the ball undetected and moved toward a footman who held a tray of bubbling champagne. And oh dear, oh dear, did she need to have a drink right at this moment.

She gained a glass and fought not to consume it like a woman dying of thirst. With a will of its own, her attention moved back toward the closet room door, and she watched as Montague stepped back into the ballroom, perfectly attired and without a hair out of place.

How was it that he could be so calm, so unflustered after what they had just done...

The pit of her stomach fluttered, and she clasped her abdomen, hoping she wasn't as rosy as she feared. Never had she ever been with a man like she had been with Montague.

He had mastered her body, played with it to his own tune, and made her sing in a way she had never thought possible.

Oh dear Lord, she would remember that closet for the rest of her days.

"Stop looking at Montague as if you're dying of thirst, Kate."

Startled at her sister's words, Kate cleared her throat and averted her gaze. "I'm not staring at the duke. Whatever do you mean?" she asked, the nervous laugh that accompanied her words giving away her lie.

"I saw you leave the closet. In fact, I watched you disappear into the room with the duke and stood nearby to ensure whatever was happening within it was not made public. Care to explain why you were in there so long?" Anwen asked her, her pointed stare telling Kate she did not want to hear anything but the truth.

But how could she tell her sister the truth without making herself feel worthless? She was his lover, his mistress...

"The duke and I are intimate, Anwen. Is that what you wish for me to tell you?" Not that Kate would tell her the details behind their arrangement or the reason they were being intimate, but Anwen could be led to believe they were merely lovers, an affair of the heart, and nothing more.

"Intimate in what way?" Anwen asked, a small frown between her brows.

"As in the way men and women are when they're alone. In bed." Kate stared ahead, unable to meet her sibling's gaze, but she heard her startled intake of breath.

"You're sleeping with the Wild Wolfe of London? However did that come about?"

Kate wanted to scream that Brassel was why such a proposition came about, but she did not. What was done was done, and there was no changing that. Not to mention, sleeping with Montague wasn't so flawed. He certainly ensured she enjoyed herself with whatever they did.

"I do not know. It just occurred. Tonight was not the

first night we've been intimate, but never have we been so daring as to be so near a party."

Anwen's eyes grew even more expansive than they were before. "You mean to tell me I just stood guard to the closet door while Montague was servicing you? Oh, my heavens, Kate. Whatever has come over you? You could be ruined. You could have been caught and found with your dress over your head."

Kate chuckled at the image her sister's words brought forth in her mind, and she shook her head. "The duke, as you know, is used to being so scandalous that I was never in danger. He would not have allowed us to be caught, I'm certain." Not that she was utterly confident the closet door had been locked, but had they been caught, a gentleman at heart, he would not have let her be ruined.

"But I was not. I merely spent several minutes alone with him, which was quite pleasurable." She turned to Anwen and threw her a consoling smile. "I'm merely having a little liaison. Nothing more, and this will not last forever. Do not worry, please. And do not tell a soul what happened. I do not need your husband or brother's involvement in my business. Promise me you will keep what you know to yourself."

Anwen appeared displeased, but she nodded, moving over to the footman and taking a glass of champagne for herself. She rejoined Kate and clicked their glasses together. "Here's to you, sister, and your newfound freedom and joy. But please be careful. Guard your heart; a man like Montague will not give his away, and as sweet, kind, and beautiful as you are, I fear he will use you and spit you out when he's had his fill."

Kate smiled, but her sister was right. Of course, Montague would spit her out when he was finished. He only wanted her for one thing: her body, not her mind or what she could offer him. A shame, for she could see the good in him, the man he could be if he were not such a rogue. It would be a spirited woman indeed who could make the Wild Wolfe of London bend a knee. A woman who would never be her.

W olfe fought to control the emotions rioting within him. He ran a hand through his hair and ventured to the gaming room, needing to remove himself from the vicinity of Kate.

The last thing he needed to do was hoist her over his shoulder and carry her out of the ball and into his carriage, where he could regain his fill of her.

Dear Lord in heaven, she was an angel, yet there was a little devilment about her that called to his wild side, made him seek more, push and tease her with a side of him that he tried to keep tame.

But she drove him to distraction.

He took a deep breath, needing to calm his racing heart. Making the gaming room, he leaned against a nearby wall and watched several gentlemen gamble their inheritances.

He would not join them this evening. His mind was all at sixes and sevens, and it would take several hours before he regained control of himself.

How could he keep away from her now that he'd had her entirely? She was exquisite, so responsive, and enjoyed his body as much as he enjoyed hers.

He swallowed and closed his eyes momentarily, reliving the image of sliding into her tight cunny. The thought of when he could do it again was forthright in his mind.

Could he escort her home? Was tonight too soon to taste her sweet lips again?

The sound of a waltz floated into the gaming room, and he turned to watch those who moved out onto the ballroom floor. The sight of Kate being swept into Lord Griffin's arms sent a shock through his body, unlike anything he'd ever known.

Not that he was her jailer and could say who she spent time with or danced with at balls and parties, but after what they had done in the closet, seeing her smiling and discussing whatever it was that had them both enthralled was...riling.

He wasn't sure if he enjoyed the sensation coursing through his veins. He refused to believe it was jealousy, but it could be annoyance, frustration that Kate seemed so unbothered by their interlude.

Unable to tear his gaze from her, he watched the dance, followed her every move up and down the large ballroom floor, and the longer he watched, the more vexed he became.

Was she so unmoved by him? Yet here he was, his heart still pumping far too fast, his skin prickling with awareness at the thought of her being in the same room. He could still smell the lily perfume on his skin, imprinted on his mind to haunt him until he bathed next.

What had happened to him? He was not the kind of man to crave a woman. He slept with many, his mistress most of all, but then he would move onward, give them what they wanted, and extradite himself without hurting anyone's feelings. A pleasurable interlude that was over before it began.

But with Kate, it was different. He felt alien when he

was with her and did not know how to work through that. Did not know if he wished to.

Lord Griffin threw Kate a wolfish smile, and he fisted his hands at his sides. How dare the bastard act the seducer with her. Did he not know she was a widow, a woman barely back in society after the death of her husband?

He ought to remind Lord Griffin of his duty as a gentleman to keep his distance from Kate and anyone else who dared dance or appeared too familiar with her.

Or better, speak to Kate and ensure she remembered that while he promised not to be intimate with others while they were completing their agreement, the same went for her.

CHAPTER
FOURTEEN

The following afternoon, Wolfe took a turn about Hyde Park in his curricle. He told himself he was there merely to enjoy the warm summer's day, take in the parklands that often reminded him of his country estate, and enjoy some time outdoors.

All lies, of course, for he was there for one thing and one thing only.

Kate...

He had spied her not long after arriving. She stood with Lady Orford and the Duchess Blackhaven, who had married his good friend, the duke.

"Oh, do take another turn, Your Grace," Lady Jacobs cooed at his side, linking her arm through his.

He ground his teeth, knowing he should not have her next to him, pushing all of Kate's annoyed buttons, but he could not help himself. After seeing her last evening dancing with Lord Griffin, a little tit-for-tat was just what he needed.

Was she sleeping with his lordship? He did not think so, but that did not mean she did not want to.

The thought turned his stomach, and he narrowed his eyes, pulling the carriage to the side of the drive and tying the reins to the chair. "Let me help you down, my lady. We'll take a stroll if you would like?" he asked, jumping down.

Her ladyship pouted, clearly wishing to remain in the vehicle, but proceeded to reach for his hand for assistance.

Lady Jacobs was a beautiful woman and widowed a year before Kate. A woman in a similar position as Kate, except Lady Jacobs had been left in the advantageous position of wealth and an heir, making marriage no longer a requirement if she did not wish.

She was the type of woman in the past he would spend a lot of time with and relish, but now, walking beside her, listening to her talk about the latest on dit, which he was surprised did not involve him, bored him almost to sleep.

Wolfe looked ahead and fought to remain attentive and engaged. He caught Kate's eye, who glanced in their direction. Hers narrowed, and had he not known every facet of her pretty features, he would have missed the turning up of her lip.

Was she annoyed? Jealous seeing him with another woman?

Still, he was keeping to his agreement. Nothing was occurring between him and Lady Jacobs. No matter if her ladyship wished it to be different, he would not engage her propositions, which totaled three already since picking her up on Mount Street.

"Duchess Blackhaven, Lady Orford, Lady Brassel, good afternoon to you all." He bowed. "You all know Lady Jacobs," he said, introducing the woman at his side to Kate's set of friends.

Each of them welcomed Lady Jacobs, all but Kate,

whose cold, hard stare made fire kindle to life within him. She was incensed. He could all but see smoke coming out of her ears.

"Lady Brassel, I hope you enjoyed the ball last evening. You certainly looked engaged in the many dances you partook," he stated, schooling his features to one of interest, not disdain.

"Do you always watch how many dances Lady Brassel enjoys, Your Grace?" the Duchess Blackhaven asked him, one curious brow raised.

He shook his head and fought not to look caught out by his own questioning. "No, of course not. I'm merely curious as I had asked her ladyship for a dance, and alas, she had denied me the pleasure," he lied, not wanting them to think he watched Kate more than he did already.

Which was too much in his estimation.

"Really, Your Grace?" Kate queried. "I do not remember you asking me to dance. How strange to learn that you did."

Strangely, Wolfe was enjoying the back-and-forth he always encountered with Lady Brassel. He had invariably known her to be an independent-thinking woman who called out liars when needed.

He bit back a grin, hoping that seeing him this afternoon with another lady reminded her that her actions with Lord Griffin the night before were noted.

She's not your wife, Wolfe. She owes you nothing.

True, he could not deny that fact, but she was his for the duration of the Season. "Very strange indeed. It was when we were unattended. Do you not remember that?"

Kate cleared her throat, her face paling at his words. A little devilment crowed that he'd bested her, but then, a part of him wondered why he wanted to tease her. Possibly cause more strife than even he wanted.

"I do not think taking the air and walking the terrace is alone as you would lead people to believe," she returned his lie with one of her own.

"Touchè," he stated, ignoring Lady Jacobs at his side, who kept glancing between him and Kate, as if to keep up with the conversation.

"Are you enjoying your outing, Lady Jacobs? It is a lovely day for a ride in the park, is it not?" Kate asked. "In fact, you should ask the duke to escort you out to Richmond one day. Another park that is very pretty this time of year."

"Oh, that would be lovely, Your Grace. Do you not think?" Lady Jacobs questioned.

Regret ran down his spine that he had ever come to speak to Kate after that little feat. Was she trying to torture him with more time with Lady Jacobs than he wanted?

You only asked her for a carriage outing to irritate Kate...

He met his nemesis's eyes and glared. "When the time permits, I can escort Lady Jacobs. Perhaps we ought to make a day of it. Several of us ride out to Richmond and enjoy a picnic," he suggested, in no way wishing to be alone with Lady Jacobs, who started staring at him as if a proposal was forthcoming. It could not be further from the truth.

Kate cleared her throat and forced an unbothered tone to mask her following words. "Oh, that would be lovely, but we would not like to intrude, Your Grace."

"There is no intrusion. I invited you all," he said, watching her. In fact, he had not moved his attention from her for several minutes. A fact that had not gone unnoticed by her friends.

The infuriating man, how dare he strut about the park

with Lady Jacobs, a woman known to enjoy her widowhood more than most women. It certainly seemed as if the duke was enjoying it as well.

Were they intimate? Had he broken their agreement?

She wanted to drag him away by his ear and ask him. The pompous, lofty fool had better not think he could trick her into thinking he had not. Why would he promenade with the lady if he were not interested in sharing her bed?

The idea of him being intimate, of kissing Lady Jacobs the way he had kissed her last evening in the closet, made her stomach churn. She did not want to imagine or hear of such a thing.

Not when all she had thought about since returning home last night was when she would see him again. Be with him as they had.

You want him. Admit it.

True, she did want him, as intimate as they had been. She wanted to feel the rapture she encountered when he'd played her body like a fine instrument, a master of his craft.

She took a calming breath. He was not the Wild Wolfe of London for nothing...

"I think that sounds like a lovely idea, Your Grace. We shall look at our appointments and events we're to attend and ensure we spend a lovely day at Richmond before the Season is over," Lady Orford said.

He nodded at her sister's words. "Lady Brassel," he said. "Will you walk with me a moment? There is a matter I would like to discuss with you regarding Lord Brassel, if you will."

She nodded and acquiesced, and he let go of Lady Jacobs to take Kate's arm. As he escorted her from the party of women, he heard them speak to Lady Jacobs and bring her into a conversation regarding Madame Dumont and her latest designs.

"What do you wish to speak to me about, Your Grace? Do you want me to allow you your way with Lady Jacobs?" Kate stated, her tone cold. "You will not get it unless you agree to end this agreement between us."

He tightened his hold on her arm, laying his hand over her soft, gloved fingers. He led them toward a copse of trees, away from the prying eyes of the *ton* who walked the paths surrounding them.

"No, I do not wish to sleep with Lady Jacobs. I have my lover next to me now. No need to include anyone else in my bed unless that is something you wish to experience."

Kate gasped, having not ever heard of such a thing. "I do not wish for that, thank you, Your Grace. And I do not even wish to imagine that you have in your wild past." Which she had no doubt he had if the knowing smirk across his features were any indication.

They moved out of sight of her friends, and without warning, he pressed her up against a tree. The scent of sandalwood drove her to distraction.

"Does it pain you to see me with Lady Jacobs? Do you wish I had called and asked you for a carriage outing?"

"Why do you need to know, Your Grace? Perhaps it is not I who needs to answer that question." Kate smirked when the smug expression left his features. "Why are you promenading all these ladies before me, Duke? Are you trying to prove to yourself that you're still a rogue? Still the Wild Wolfe of London?" She chuckled. "More like a puppy dog if I were to term you as any animal."

FIFTEEN

Kate steeled herself to be strong, not to give way to the rioting emotions within her. She did not care what he did. His being at the park today was all for show. To tell her yet again that he was in control, pulled the strings of whatever was happening between them.

"I know nothing is happening between you and Lady Jacobs, and I know this because if it were so, we would no longer have an agreement, and I would be free of you."

"And is that what you want?" he asked, towering over her.

Kate laid her hands on his chest, a mistake the moment she did so, for her fingers instinctively curled into his waist-coat, feeling the taut muscles beneath her palms.

Oh, how lovely he felt. All hard, muscular, strong man that was hers to have whenever she wanted. "Maybe you ought to ask yourself that question, Your Grace. You are the one who's escorting a lady to the park."

He closed the space between them, pushing them farther into the copse of trees. Her back bumped into a tall elm, and she met his eyes, watched as his darkened with a hunger that matched her own.

She should not feel the way she did. She should not allow him to have so much power over her, but alas, she could not help herself. She hated the games he played, the flaunting of other women when she was chastised for dancing with a friend.

The man had never not once gained his way. She should leave, push past him, teach him a lesson...

A muscle worked in his jaw, and he reached for her, cupping her face. "Right now, all I want to do is kiss you."

Kate could almost allow herself to sink into his sweet words. Tumble hard for the desire that radiated from him and all for her, but she could not. This was all a game. She meant nothing to him but a means to an end.

"We could be seen."

He dipped his head, so his words whispered against her lips. "I do not care."

Kate gasped as his mouth covered hers, taking her lips in a searing kiss. A kiss that left her head spinning and her knees weak. She fisted the lapels of his coat in her hands and kept him near, even when a cantering horse sounded nearby.

His tongue tangled with hers, his strong hand slipping about her nape and tipping her head to deepen the embrace. All Kate could do was hold on to him, stop herself from pooling into a puddle of desire at his feet. Never had she been kissed so passionately and so publicly.

Not that anyone could see, but if they were alone for much longer, it would certainly raise questions.

But even with all of that dashing through her mind, she did not stop. She continued to seek, taste, and enjoy his hard, commanding kiss that was everything she had ever wanted.

He wrenched out of her hold and strode away with a determination like their kiss. Kate stumbled and caught the tree to stabilize herself.

She touched her lips, sure they were a little swollen. She leaned against the tree for a time, fighting to control her racing heart. The man was a menace, and to leave her here, not even escort her back, why, he really did wish to have a shouting match.

Kate left the copse of trees when she was sure her equilibrium was as it should be and was pleased to find her friends waiting for her with no sign of the duke.

"His Grace bid you good afternoon, Kate," Anwen said, her sister's gaze pinned upon her lips.

Kate fought not to touch her mouth, hoping it was not swollen or red. Surely, the ladies would not think anything untoward had occurred when they had taken the short stroll.

"Perhaps he means to make Lady Jacobs his wife," Kate said, hoping to turn the attention off of her and onto someone else—namely the duke and his lady friend.

"I do not think Lady Jacobs will ever marry. She may play with the duke as much as he will play with her, but that will be the end of it. I do not think he will marry at all," the Duchess Blackhaven said, looking in the direction where the duke had departed.

The thought of Montague never marrying made the pit of her stomach churn. For all his wayward, wicked ways, to remain alone, childless, grow old without anyone by his side did not sit well with Kate. Although she had not thought about marrying again, should she fall in love, she would give up the little freedom she now had to have a husband.

The idea of marrying the duke herself floated through her mind, and as much as she fought against the idea when he kissed her the way he just had, the idea of living without such passion for the rest of her life seemed like a torment.

Not that he would marry her. He said himself that he would be off to Scotland with his mistress the moment the Season was over. And as passionate and all-consuming as his kisses were, that did not equate to love.

And she would not marry unless love was the main ingredient in her future. She could not endure another four years of mediocre friendship and nothing more. Living like that once was enough.

M ontague dropped Lady Jacobs at her home and helped her ladyship alight from the carriage. "Thank you for joining me today, my lady. I enjoyed myself immensely, and I will be in contact regarding our trip to Richmond," he said, willing to play the gentleman a little longer.

Her ladyship stepped against him, heedless of those walking on Mount Street on which they stood.

Wolfe looked around, hoping no one could see her advances, and was thankful that no one was present so far.

"Are you not going to come up, Your Grace? After your little promenade with Lady Brassel, I thought you may be eager for release." Her hand reached between them and cupped his cock.

A man, and one who fought desire most of his days, felt nothing at her touch. His cock typically had a mind of its own, standing to attention at the worst times, but not today, it would seem.

Although when he'd been in the copse of trees with Kate, his cock had pressed against his falls so hard he'd been sure the buttons keeping him in check would pop.

He'd like nothing more than to be standing here with Kate, having her hands on his person instead.

"That's it, Montague. Get hard for me and come inside. Let us have a pleasurable afternoon together."

He stepped out of her hold, thinking about how to explain the movement in his pants, not by her, but the very thought of Kate. Somehow, in the past few days, she'd embedded herself into his soul, and he was unsure if he'd ever have enough of her.

"I beg your pardon, but I have a long overdue appointment with my steward." He clasped her hand and placed it on his arm, walking her up the three steps to her door. "I bid you a good afternoon, Lady Jacobs," he said, kissing her gloved hand and removing himself from her person.

He climbed into his curricle, flicked the reins to his matched bays, and started toward Berkeley Square. Surely, by now, Kate would be home after her stroll in the park.

The day was warm, and he was certain ladies did not like to stay out in the sun too long for fear of gaining freckles.

It took him only a short time through the streets of Mayfair to arrive at her residence, and he drove his carriage to the mews at the back of the house. He had promised her secrecy, and he would attempt that at all costs. By the time he ambled to the square, he observed her friend's carriage rolling away and Kate entering the house.

He waited several minutes to ensure no one was about before he knocked on the door. Her footman, a man of similar age to Wolfe, answered and took his card before walking upstairs.

Wolfe kicked his heels in the foyer before movement at the top of the stairs caught his attention. He fought to keep the breath in his lungs at the sight of Kate, changed into a soft-blue afternoon gown, one that was for lounging around at home and when one did not expect callers.

She looked like springtime, the color of her gown reminding him of a clear summer sky. Her cheeks blossomed into a light, rosy hue, and he would do anything to know what she was thinking right at this moment.

"What are you doing here, Montague?" she asked, not moving from her position.

Well, if she would not come down to see him, he would merely have to go upstairs to see her. He ascended the stairs, meeting her at the top. "I had to see you again," he admitted, but no more. He would not tell her that he did not know himself around her. It was such a foreign way of living and one he was not used to in the slightest.

He was not the type of man to long for a woman. Certainly not one woman. And yet, what he wanted, he knew he could only gain from the one woman standing before him.

"You cannot be here. It's the middle of the day," she argued.

He chuckled, forgetting that she thought lovemaking could only occur at night. "Well," he said, taking her hand and walking up the passage to where he hoped her rooms were situated. "Time to prove to you that lovemaking can be accomplished during daylight hours and that you'll enjoy it just as much as you would if it were dark."

CHAPTER
SIXTEEN

"Lady Brassel, Master Oliver is awake now. Would you like me to take him into your private parlor?" her son's nurse asked from the end of the corridor, pulling hers and Montague's attention.

She turned to Miss Denning and nodded. "Yes, thank you. I will join you momentarily." Kate watched Montague as his attention followed her son's progress up the passage before losing sight of him when he entered the parlor.

"I did not think your son was in London?" he asked, a slight frown between his brows. "Is there a reason he's here?"

"I received word from Miss Denning that he had a slight fever last week, and I asked them to travel to London to be nearer to my doctor. The Brassel estate, as you know, is in Kent, and although there is a doctor in the village, he's not as young as he once was and tends to ignore a mother's concern as nothing more than hysteria."

"Ah, I see."

Kate watched him and debated inviting him in to meet her son. Would he like to? Did he even tolerate children?

This was not part of their arrangement, and she was under no illusion that he had called on her here for another reason entirely, but still, maybe he would join her for a cup of tea and conversation. It did not always have to be sex between them. Surely, it did not.

"Would you join me, Your Grace? Oliver is the sweetest boy, and he would enjoy meeting a duke, I'm certain."

"I, ah..." Montague hedged, taking a step back. "I do not think that would be wise, my lady. I do not play with children."

Kate chuckled and started toward the parlor. "Well, no one asked you to play, merely to meet Oliver. I'm having afternoon tea with him, and you're welcome to join us."

Kate continued into the room, biting down the small glimmer of hope that he would follow and join them. The duke's hesitant steps faltered at the door, and she sat on a nearby settee, reaching for Oliver.

"Thank you, Miss Denning, for bringing him to me. You may have your break now," she suggested, tickling her son when he wiggled on her lap.

She heard the duke clear his throat at the door, and Kate looked up, smiling. "Your Grace, may I introduce you to Lord Oliver Brassel. Oliver, darling," she said, pointing toward the duke. "This is His Grace, the Duke of Montague, and a good friend to your papa."

Her son looked toward the duke and at two years of age, did not comprehend who his father was or what friendship was for that matter, having been only one when George died.

"Hello," her son said, remembering at least a little of the etiquette he was being taught.

"Very good, Oliver. You could also say, Good afternoon, Your Grace."

Oliver watched her lips, and she could see he was listening. Such a good-natured little boy. She hoped she could always protect and raise him right so nothing would ever harm or hurt him.

"Good afternoon, Your Grace," he said, looking to her for clarification that he had done as she asked.

"Well done, Oliver. That was perfect."

The duke came and sat on a nearby wingback chair, crossing his legs.

"You know you do not have to look so fierce," she said, letting Oliver wiggle off her lap to play with some wooden bricks always kept in a basket nearby.

The duke uncrossed his legs and attempted to appear relaxed. Not very convincingly, he was so broad, such a tall, muscular man that he never seemed to be at ease.

She drank in his appearance, not entirely at ease herself that he was sitting in her parlor while her son played at their feet. The Wild Wolfe of London did not do such homely measures ever.

"Is this better?" he asked, his voice deep and gravelly, making her stomach flip.

"Yes, much better."

His gaze took in her every feature, darkened with some emotion she could not make out and wasn't entirely sure she wanted to. Not right at this moment, anyway. She would debate what had happened between them today when she was alone in her bed tonight where, scandalously, she could relive every word, touch, and look he bestowed on her, sending her heart racing and her body burning with need.

The man was dangerous in more ways than one.

Oliver went up to the duke and handed him a block before going back to pick up another to show him. Kate held her breath as the duke took in her son and the block he gave him before lifting it up and inspecting it himself. "It is a fine block, Master Oliver. Do you know how many you have?" the duke asked her son.

Oliver's eyes widened before he went over and started collecting all the blocks and placing them in the basket, which then, too, was carried over to the duke to show him.

"I have lots," her son mumbled, pointing out a dog, cat, fish, or whatever animal was painted on the different sides.

"And what is this animal?" the duke asked Oliver.

For several minutes, she watched as Oliver and Montague discussed the many creatures on her son's blocks, and her heart skipped a beat. Her little boy missed having a father, and she was sad that George was not here to raise him or see him grow into the fine man she was determined he become.

To see the duke take an interest, to play and even smile a time or two at her boy made the lump in her throat grow.

"You are good with children, Your Grace. A surprising find that I did not think was possible for you."

He leaned back in his chair, holding the basket of blocks as her son walked over to a small bookcase and pulled out a handful of his favorite stories.

"He looks like you. Oliver has the same eyes as you do." He met her eyes, and something in his gaze made her want to crawl onto his lap, squeeze the rake out of him, and make him how she wished he could be.

A gentleman courting her, falling for her, loving her as she deserved. Not the other man who was sleeping with her as a means for her to pay a debt.

His actions today, his sweetness around her son, did not suit whom he portrayed. Was he really just a rake? A man who sought pleasure and nothing more from the fairer sex? It could not be so.

"He's the sweetest boy, and I thank you for saying such a lovely thing about his looks. I want to think he has a little of me in him. People always say he looks like Brassel, and I sometimes wonder if they remember that I birthed him at all."

"He does not look like Brassel. He's entirely yours, even right down to his sweet nose."

Sweet nose? Kate fought not to react to his words that were as charming as he said her nose was.

He cleared his throat and was spared saying anything further when a footman brought in tea and small sandwiches.

"Would you like a cup?" she asked, pouring herself and Oliver one, as was their practice.

"Yes, thank you."

Kate poured him tea and handed him the cup and saucer. His fingers grazed hers as he took the cup, and a shiver of awareness ran up her arm. Seeing him in a situation of domesticity was something she did not need to muddle her mind even further, but alas, here they were.

Oliver came over and, ignoring his cup of tea, started toward the duke. Kate watched, wondering what His Grace would do. Would he try to distract her son to return to his books or suggest that the blocks by his feet needed further examining?

Her son lifted his arms, a sign he wanted to be picked up, and without looking to her for guidance, Montague set down his cup of tea and picked up Oliver without a flicker of annoyance.

She felt the lump in her throat return, the prickling of tears as the duke explained different articles of clothing he was wearing. Oliver settled onto his lap, handing Montague the small book he held, and the duke took his cue and started reading about a mouse who lived in a field.

She sat back in her chair, allowing the softer melody of Montague's voice to wash over her. He made a charming sight, a sight she never thought ever to see. A man, reading to a small boy, a domesticated scene that broke her heart that it was all an illusion. A day that was unlikely to occur again, no matter how much she may wish it otherwise.

Kate did not dare interrupt or state how well the duke appeared reading to a child. A father figure for a moment. She doubted he would appreciate the compliment and would likely bolt at the mere thought he was falling into that trap.

The duke's voice took on the tone of a disgruntled toad telling off the field mouse, and her son giggled. The duke smiled, and the breath in her lungs seized. She'd never seen him smile in such a wholesome, innocent way.

Guard your heart, Kate. He's not the marrying kind. Not the type of man who'll be a father to your son.

But oh, how she wished things could be different between them. Even if they could be friends one day, where there was nothing more between them other than to help guide her son.

He looked up and caught her eyes, and her heart thumped hard in her chest. She knew she could never be just friends with the man before her. They were well past that, even if he did not know it yet.

CHAPTER
SEVENTEEN

"I believe your son has fallen asleep," Wolfe said, the little boy's body growing heavier by the minute. He lay wilted in his arms, the book they were reading laying over his small chest.

Kate chuckled and watched him. Her eyes sparkled with humor and something else he could not place but may have probably guessed what she was thinking.

That he was reformed, that being with her today had altered who he was at his core. Of course, little Oliver was sweet, and he enjoyed spending time with Kate and her son, but that did not mean he was changed or would convert for her or anyone.

Some would question why he was so determined to remain alone for the rest of his life. He did not wish to marry and beget heirs, marry a woman who promised love and fidelity only to win a duchess coronet. For years, he had attended marriage after marriage that ended in heartache. Husbands growing bored with their wives. Wives who, in turn, loathed their husbands for their inability to remain steadfast and faithful.

Kate's marriage was no exception to this. A union formed out of duty and necessity. Kate wishing to secure her future in society, and Brassel wanting a pretty wife on his arm. No love or affection ever part of the contract.

He had stepped aside for Brassel, watched as she accepted his mediocre affections, gleefully playing the besotted debutante, and all the time, he knew it to be a lie.

She had not loved George any more than he loved his mistress. She tolerated him at best, and she had agreed to marry his friend, accepted his terms, and left Wolfe... discontented and more than ever determined not to fall into that situation, no matter his duty to the duchy or not.

Little Oliver's hand gripped the lapel of his coat as he moved, his small mouth opening with a yawn before he went back to sleep.

"I should ring for the nurse and have her take him up to his room." Kate stood and came over to him. She leaned down and picked up her son.

Their proximity near, Wolfe caught the sweet lily scent that accompanied her everywhere. With a child in her arms, she seemed even more beautiful than he had seen her.

"Master Oliver is a delight, Kate. You ought to be proud."

A light blush stole across her cheeks as she rocked Oliver in her arms. "He is the dearest little boy. I'm so fortunate to have him." She watched her son, a wistful smile on her lips.

He knew the look well. His mother, having been a doting mama, had often looked upon him in such a way before she passed.

A lump formed in his throat, and he swallowed.

Hard.

What the hell was that? He had not thought of his

mother in years and did not expect to feel emotional about losing her. He was but sixteen when she died—more than enough time had passed for him to mourn her. He was, after all, almost seven and twenty.

"It is a shame that George did not know Oliver as well as he should have before he passed. But as you know, he was often busy, and his duties in town left little time for family life."

Wolfe stood and rang the bell for a servant. "Why did you marry Brassel if you did not love him?" he blurted without thought.

Surprise registered on her face before she thought about his question. "He asked me, and I did not want to burden my family by remaining a spinster any longer. I was one of the oldest debutantes of the Season. I could not remain drifting between Anwen's and Domonic's houses. They had their own lives to live, nevertheless putting up with a sister who could not find a match."

"So you did not love him?" he asked. He should not question her so, but he needed to know. What made women settle? Why did she not wait for others who had shown interest?

Namely him...

"I liked him very much, and I love that he gave me Oliver, but shamefully, no, I did not love him. But George did not love me either, so there was little I could be upset about. He gave me a pleasing, comfortable home. He was titled and rich. I should never be a burden to my family as his wife." She met his eyes, and he read the annoyance in her blue stare. "What would you have me do if I did not marry Brassel? Maybe I could have been a companion, or when my family was done with me, an old aunt who watches their children while they enjoy the Season? Or perhaps I could have gone into trade, sewing dresses for the *ton*. Is that what you wish for me? I cannot go to university like you, Your Grace. I could not build my own life, for it is not done for well-bred young ladies. All I could do was marry, and so I accomplished that goal. I will not have you judge me for that. Not when you're rutting about London, practically a male whore."

Wolfe gaped just as a light knock sounded on the door and the nurse he had seen earlier entered. "You called, Lady Brassel?" she asked.

"Yes, thank you, Miss Denning. You may take Oliver up to his room. He's fallen asleep, as you can see."

The young woman came and collected Oliver and left without fuss, leaving them alone.

"A male whore? Well, I'm glad to know that is what you think of me." Not that he could quite believe she had said what she did, but nor could he refute it. He had slept with many women, too many to count, and possibly women whom Kate was acquainted with.

He enjoyed women as much as wine, and both were excessive at times.

But hearing it from her—from Kate—well, it irked and stabbed at a part of him he did not know beat in his chest.

"I apologize. I should not have said that." Kate bustled about the room, picking up blocks and placing the few books Oliver had pulled out of the bookcase back where they belonged.

"No, I apologize. I should not have questioned you on your choices."

An overwhelming urge to rail at him, to make him see that women did not have all the opportunities that men did, coiled within her, but she did not. What would be the point? He would not understand even if she did try to explain her choices any more than she already had.

"My choices may have been different had you been in the park that day. Instead, you sent your friend to escort me on our promenade. You could have been honest if you were not interested in me."

The duke ran a hand through his hair, staring at her with a look that she could not place. Was he conflicted? Did he wish to tell her something that she did not already know?

He glanced at the floor, and a muscle worked in his jaw before he spoke. "You have no idea how much I wanted to accompany you to the park that day. Of course, as a young, foolish man then, I believed that women would follow their hearts over their pocketbooks, but alas, I was wrong. I gave over to Brassel when he begged me to step aside. I agreed to allow him to court you instead, for he was my friend and had not had much luck with women, until you, of course."

Kate felt her heart skip a beat hearing his words. Had he stepped aside? For George? "I did not think you were interested, so I did not seek you out after you rescinded our stroll. George said you called on Miss Bertie instead and asked him to walk with me so I would not be disappointed."

"The bastard. I never called on Miss Bertie. For one, she was terribly bad-tempered toward her own sex, and second, she resembled a pug."

Kate bit her lip, fighting the urge to giggle. "I did not know you allowed George to court me instead of you. Why did you not try to win my hand if that is what you wanted back then? Our life now could be so very different."

For one, she would be with a man who sparked so much feeling within her that she sometimes did not know what to do with it. He made her crave, want to shout how delicious he was from the rooftops, and rail at him for being a stubborn, stick-in-the-mud.

"Promenading with you does not equal marriage, Kate. You're getting ahead of yourself."

But was she? Was some of the resentment he bore toward her out of annoyance at himself for having not pursued her when he could? Was he annoyed at her for marrying George and forgetting the little hope she once held that she had captured the duke's attention?

"Am I?" she questioned, sauntering over to him. She reached up and clasped the lapels of his jacket. The duke's eyes widened, and she felt every muscle tense within him. "If you wanted me, then you should have fought for me. Not given over so easily merely to please a friend."

His eyes narrowed, and she saw he was weighing her words and what to say next. Would he agree? Or remain steadfast in his ways and deny he'd ever felt anything for her.

Which begged the question. Could he feel anything for her again? Or would he walk away from what was happening between them out of pride? Out of his determination to remain the Wild Wolfe of London.

Wild indeed. Even the most undomesticated cat could be tamed with love, affection, and time if one was willing.

Are you willing, Kate?

"Is it a fault to be loyal to a friend?" he asked, his voice deep and gravelly.

She stepped against him and wrapped her arms around

his neck. The feel of his body, hard, warm, and hers to do with as she pleased, sent a thrill to her core, warming her in all the appetizing places.

"Not a fault, but something to be commended, no matter how wrong you were," she said, sealing her statement with a kiss.

EIGHTEEN

Damn everything to hell. What was happening to him? He was a rogue, a rakehell, a womanizer, and possibly what Kate had called him earlier, a bit of a whore when it came to the fairer sex, so why was he admitting to wanting her for himself all those years ago?

It did little for him now. He didn't want to marry and did not see the urgency when he had distant relatives who were more than capable of continuing the ducal line.

Even with all those thoughts rushing about in his mind, his arms cradled Kate against him, and he was lost. Was she still kissing him out of obligation to the debt, or was she in his arms because she wished to kiss him and often?

His pride would not allow him to ask, but the question hammered against his skull.

The kiss deepened, and his mind calmed from his thoughts, leaving only one obligation: pleasing Kate. He swept her into his arms and sat on the nearby settee, laying her over his legs.

She giggled, the sound warming his dark soul, and he

grinned through the kiss, the lure to hear such a sweet sound again overwhelming his senses.

"I think it's time we ticked off a few more items on my expectation list."

She met his eyes, a question in hers. "What are your suggestions?" she asked, not fleeing from his lap, which he half-expected.

She would indeed flee if she knew his thoughts, some of which included taking her over the settee, tasting her sweet pussy, or, if she were so brave, having her take him in her mouth.

The thought made his cock stand to attention. "I'm going to make you come, but you cannot scream or make a sound. The door is open, Lady Brassel. We do not wish for the servants to see."

Her attention moved past him to the door, which was indeed ajar. "Let me close it, and then we can be alone."

Did she mean what she said? Why did he care so much if she did? She was a widow, a woman not looking to marry any more than he was.

Enjoy your time with her, Wolfe, and be done with it.

"No one will see. The settee has its back to the door, and you'll sit beside me. No one will suspect."

She frowned, and without further ado, he lifted her off his lap and set her at his side. "Lean against the side of the chair and lift one of your legs. I'm going to touch you, Kate."

Her mouth opened with a silent sigh, and she did as he asked, even going so far as to lift her skirts, giving him a view of her ankle. "Like this?" she asked.

"Perfect." Wolfe circled her ankle with his hand, squeezing her calf before teasing the back of her knee. She squirmed and bit her lip.

"Am I allowed to make any noise at all? What you're doing is tickling me."

He inwardly growled. She would feel a lot more pleasure than mere tickling soon enough. "No, no noise at all. We must appear perfectly composed as if we're sitting beside one another."

"You know that I will not be able to do that. When you touch me, you know that I cannot control my reactions."

Her words were music to his ears. One part of him longed to have her, to win her as he'd once desired more than anything else. But then another side of him wanted to use her up, enjoy her, and then walk away, sated and alone as he always was.

No commitments. Not a concern in the world.

Except nights and days filled with busy nothings.

"You will have to try." He reached the ties of her silk stockings and slipped a finger beneath one. Her skin was softer than he remembered, and he teased her flesh for several minutes, touching ever closer to her apex.

She squirmed, seeking his hand, and he knew she understood what he would do to her. His fingers brushed her mons, a featherlight touch before he swirled his middle finger at her wet core.

Kate closed her eyes and lifted a little off the seat, seeking his touch. He gave her what she wanted, what they both wanted. He slipped one finger, then two into her wet, hot heat and fucked her like he'd wanted from the moment he saw her in the park.

Her hands flexed on the settee, gripping the gold silk covering, her eyes fluttering closed with each stroke of his hand.

"Tell me you like it. Tell me I've only ever been the one to please you, so..."

She made a little mewling sound that went straight to his groin, and he regretted his idea of not allowing them more privacy. He'd do anything to sink into her sweet heat. To please them both with a good, hard fucking.

"I love you touching me. I should not, but I do."

Her words sparked a fire in him and bedamned the ajar door. He had to kiss, touch, and bring her to release, and he did not care who watched.

Kate gasped as he came up against her, taking her lips in a searing kiss that left her breathless and her head spinning.

She reached for him, and his hand played between her legs with expertise. He swirled his thumb against her flesh, taking her with his fingers, and each time, she drew closer and closer to the exquisite release she knew he could give her.

"Wolfe, what about you?" she asked, reaching for his cock. It was large, hard as a rock, and strained against his falls. She rubbed him, feeling him grow even more, and heat pooled between her legs.

"You want me," he asked, nibbling her bottom lip.

"I do. I want you inside me." She had never admitted to such a desire before but could not lie. Somewhere between agreeing to repay Brassel's debt and now, she had come to crave the man in her arms.

She wanted to please him. Have him please her in return. The thought of him taking anyone to his bed after they parted made her lips curl in disgust.

Was she the only person who sensed whatever was starting between them? She was not so blind, so naïve not to know when they had shifted past merely fucking, as he called it, to lovemaking.

Not that she had ever experienced lovemaking in her life. Brassel certainly did not touch her the way Wolfe was doing now. Her skin prickled in awareness when he was around, and her heart raced. She looked for him at balls and parties and should not. He occupied too much of her thoughts, and then after today with her son...

What could she do when he was utterly perfect with her little boy? So kind and patient. She had not thought he would be so, but maybe he had even surprised himself with his sweetness.

How could she not fall under the spell of such a man? How was she to get the Wild Wolfe of London to succumb to feelings, to acknowledge that she meant more to him than a quick tumble behind closed doors?

"Turn around and lean over the chair's armrest. I want you," he admitted. "I cannot wait."

Could she hope that his words had a double meaning? That he wanted her physically and emotionally? How could she win a man's heart who was so determined to remain alone and aloof for the rest of his life?

Kate did as he asked, and a moment later, cool air kissed the backs of her legs. He pressed against her, his fingers guiding his manhood into her from behind.

She had never been taken in such a position. She clutched the silk armrest, savoring the feel of him entering her, his manhood stretching, enticing, filling her with satisfaction.

Kate moaned, unable to hold back the satisfaction of having him deep within her.

"You feel so good, Kate," he whispered against her ear, thrusting into her with a fierce determination.

She met his every plunge, pressed back as he thrust forward. With every stroke, her body tightened and thrummed—the need within her building.

His hand tickled her lower belly, dipping farther, his thumb rolled the sensitive place between her legs.

She gasped, held his hand against her cunny, and kept him there, not wanting him to stop. Their lovemaking was frantic, with quick thrusts and muffled moans.

"I'm going to come. Tell me that you're close," he gasped. "Jesus, Kate, you undo me."

"I'm close. Please, please do not stop," she begged, the need encompassing her and bringing her to a maddening juncture.

And then she felt the first contractions of her release, a wave of pleasure that grew stronger and more substantial as he continued his relentless taking of her from behind.

"Wolfe," she gasped, his hand covering her mouth to quiet her sobs.

But she did not care who heard, did not care in the least if they were caught. Her body and her mind focused exclusively on pleasure, and having Wolfe share in that delight was paramount.

"Kate," he moaned. He hardened further as his release swept through him.

Kate reveled in the aftermath of satisfaction. Her body felt as light as air, floating in bliss unlike she'd ever known.

He pulled out, and she could hear him buttoning his falls and righting his clothes. Kate settled her gown back over her legs and righted herself on the chair. He busied himself with his cravat and would not look at her.

"Will I see you at the Conners ball this evening?" she asked, hoping he would attend. It was already too many hours before she would see him again.

Careful, Kate. Guard your heart. He's not the man for you... Not yet, at least.

"I will be in attendance," he said, throwing her a fleeting glance. "I will see you then. Good day to you." He strode from the room without a backward glance.

Kate sat with a small grin on her lips. He may flee, but she had seen a flicker of vulnerability in the depths of his blue eyes. A spark of unease and confusion as to what was happening between them, but she knew what it was.

Affection.

And maybe, if she were a fanciful person, it could be the start of something wonderful.

CHAPTER
NINETEEN

Three days later, Kate received an invitation to an outing at Richmond hosted by the Duke of Montague. The little note included information on what to bring, how long they would be out, and the number of people included in the party who would enjoy the day out of London.

Kate flipped the note over, hoping for a little message from the duke, but nothing was forthcoming. He had not attended the Conners ball as agreed after his visiting her here three days before. Nor had she heard a word from him, other than this invitation.

The man was a menace, and she knew his game. He disliked that she made him feel emotions he hadn't in years, or possibly for the first time in his life, and was running from her.

Coward.

She would not allow him to get away. Agreement and debt aside, she enjoyed spending time with Wolfe. He made her feel alive and gave her hope for the future, and she would not allow him to cast her aside merely because he believed his bachelorhood was paramount.

Not when she felt that was no longer the case.

He had feelings for her, and he needed to own up to them.

"Your carriage is ready, my lady."

Kate turned to the footman and set down the invitation. "Thank you, John, and can you have the carriage readied for tomorrow at nine? I'm traveling out to Richmond. Have the cook prepare a picnic basket with wine."

"Of course, my lady."

Kate left the house. This evening, she was attending Lord and Lady Finch's ball on Grosvenor Square, an event that was one of the largest, and most sought-after regarding invitations.

She took her footman's hand and allowed him to help her climb the carriage stairs. Kate settled her gown about her legs, and sat back, the short trip to Grosvenor Square a moment to compose and ready herself to see Montague.

Would he attend? Would he be sociable or cold and aloof as he often was when protecting his heart? Kate's stomach fluttered with nerves, and not for the first time in as many days, the inklings of an upset stomach made her wince.

She ought not to be anxious. The worst that could happen was she would form an attachment to the duke that was not reciprocated, whether she believed he had sentiments for her or not.

Kate clasped her abdomen and took a deep breath. Her nerves were unfounded. All would be well. She did not need to marry the duke. Her life was secure thanks to little Oliver taking over the Brassel Earldom. She looked out the window and waved to several people, making the short walk to the Finch's ball by foot. The Season had only several weeks left, and Montague would soon be off to Scotland.

She merely needed to raise her hopes with him and let him know that she would like their arrangement to last more than the Season. Would it be so bad that he knew she enjoyed his company and wished for it to continue? It would not be the world's end should he learn her truth.

The carriage rolled to a halt before the large London townhouse, and she exited the equipage, merging into the long line to greet the host and hostess before joining the ball.

Upon making the ballroom, Kate spied Anwen watching the door for her arrival and waved her over to her side. Kate bussed her sister's cheeks and took a welcome glass of champagne Anwen had secured.

"I wondered when you would arrive. I fear the room will soon be a crush, and I would not be able to find you."

Kate nodded, taking a sip of the bubbly, refreshing beverage. "Will you walk with me to the terrace? I wish to speak to you for a moment."

"Of course." Anwen linked her arm with Kate, and they headed outdoors. The terrace was bustling with guests. They made their way down to the lawns to stroll one of the many paths lit with lanterns.

"What is troubling you, Kate?" Anwen asked. "I can see that something is amiss."

Kate sighed, staring up at the stars a moment before she spoke. "I did not intend ever to tell you what I'm about to disclose, so please do not overreact when I do. But I must tell someone, for I need advice."

Anwen spied a stone seat nearby, and they sat. "You have my promise that I shall not cause a scene. Tell me what is bothering you."

Kate paused a moment, gathering her thoughts. "Well, as you know, I'm in an intimate relationship with Montague. And with each day that passes, I feel myself falling further and further under his charms." She paused, looking about to ensure privacy. "He is maddening, argumentative, and commanding at times, which I do not always agree with, but he is also sweet and makes me long for a future I may not gain. He is a wonderful lover and I do not wish for our arrangement to end."

"Why does it need to end?" Anwen asked, a slight frown between her brows.

"Because it was only ever meant to be fleeting. You do not know that Brassel owed Montague a large sum, and I suggested that because I could not pay the thousand pounds, I would repay the debt by joining him in bed."

"Kate!" Anwen reeled back, aghast. "You whored yourself?" she whispered vehemently. "Why did you not come to Orford or our brother? Both of whom would have given you the funds."

"I did not want to burden them both further. I have already overstayed my welcome at both houses."

Anwen let out a disgruntled gasp. "That is not true at all, and it pains me to think you believe you are a burden. And this absurd arrangement ends tonight. I shall have Orford and Dom pay half the fee each. No sister of mine will be a man's lover to pay off a debt. What were you thinking?"

Kate sighed, not sure she had been thinking at all. "I do not know. I wanted him, I suppose, without knowing I did, if that makes any sense at all. I wanted to enjoy a fleeting moment in the Wild Wolfe of London's bed, but now I'm all befuddled about everything. I want more of him than just a tumble for a Season. I want him in all ways. I want him to love me as I fear I have fallen for him."

"You've fallen in love with the duke?" Anwen looked at her with pity, and Kate understood the regard in her sister's eyes. The duke was not the marrying kind. Not once had he admitted to feeling more for her than sexual appetites. She may have wanted him to be more emotionally attached, but that did not make it so.

"Perhaps I have. I do not know for certain. But I do know that I no longer see our arrangement as a chore, as something I must do, but something I want to do. Please tell me that does not make me a bad person, Anwen. I feel wretched about it, truly, but I cannot help myself."

Anwen took her hands and squeezed them. "He is a handsome man, there is no doubt, but guard your heart until you know he loves you. He must admit to this himself, and if he truly has feelings for you, he will court you and seek you out even after the debt is settled."

"And if he does not?" Kate asked, not wanting to know the answer to that question. Not really. To think that he would turn about and never look in her direction again left a gaping wound in her heart.

To feel his touch, hear his wickedly sensual voice whisper naughty things in her ears. To have him play her like a fine instrument, his ability a master of his art. To interact, play, and love her son? Raise him as his own.

How could she live without such a life? Without him?

"I'm not sure I could ever repay Orford or Dom the money owed. Truly, I can endure until the end of the Season. As I said, scandalous or not, I'm enjoying my time with the duke."

"It is not right, Kate, and you should not have to abide such an obligation with a man who could leave you ruined.

No, the debt will be paid before the end of the week, and you'll be done with him, in that regard at least. And if he has feelings for you, I'm certain he will seek you out." Anwen clasped her cheek. "He would be a fool not to see the jewel before him, offering him a future much brighter than the one he now lives in."

Kate smiled. "Very well, I shall allow Orford and Dom to pay the debt, and I thank you for your help. I suppose I shall have to tell the duke this evening what to expect from them both."

"Yes, that would be best, and I wish you well." Anwen nodded toward the terrace. Kate looked up, and her eyes met with the duke's. He stood with a crystal goblet of whisky, observing them both.

"He's here," Kate said, even though she knew Anwen was already aware.

"Go and speak to him, Kate. Remember who you are, and do not allow him to have all the power over you. It is time the duke made a choice. Let us hope he makes the right one."

Kate nodded. Desiring the same but not expecting a miracle. The Wild Wolfe of London was not known to change his mind, and she doubted he would start now.

CHAPTER
TWENTY

Wolfe sauntered down to where Lady Orford and Kate sat on the stone bench in the Finch's garden—having been unable to locate Kate at the ball earlier. An unsettled feeling rooted in his gut that she may not have attended or was avoiding him.

He had been absent from several balls and parties due to an overdue meeting with his steward, who had come down from his Derbyshire estate to see him.

As much as he would not admit it to Kate or anyone, he had yearned to see her again. To have her in his arms, his to touch and kiss whenever he fancied.

Seeing her in the gardens, the moonlight kissing her dark hair, giving the curls a silvery hue made his need for her double.

However was he to remove himself from London and leave her behind?

He pushed the uncomfortable thought aside, not wanting to think of such things, not yet, at least. There were several weeks left of the Season. Indeed, by the end of his time here in London, he would have had his fill of her and be ready to remove himself from society.

Do not lie to yourself, Wolfe. The thought is revolting.

"Lady Orford, Lady Brassel," he said, bowing.

Kate and Lady Orford stood and curtsied to him. "Good evening, Your Grace," Lady Orford said, her tone chillier than usual. "I must return indoors, but I wish you a pleasant evening."

He nodded and waited for them to be alone before speaking. "Your sister, I fear, is displeased with me." He linked Kate's arm with his and started for the terrace. "Should I know what is troubling her?"

Kate pursed her lips, and he could see she debated telling him what she knew. He allowed the silence to stretch, not wishing to force it out of her or make her disclose things that were none of his business.

"There is something you should know, and I'm certain you will be pleased," Kate said, halting him before he joined the terrace where several couples strolled, and a group of gentlemen partook in a cheroot or two.

"If it is to please me, then I'm all ears," he said, curious now more than ever. She bit her lip, and he narrowed his eyes, steeling himself for whatever she told him. Not entirely confident that he would be gladdened by her disclosure, not when she appeared nervous all of a sudden.

"Lord Orford and my brother, Lord Astoridge, shall pay my husband's debt. You should have the thousand pounds before the end of the week." She threw him a small smile, and yet he did not miss that the gesture did not reach her eyes. "Are you not pleased, Your Grace? You shall be free of me and have the monetary prize you wanted all along."

Wolfe schooled his features, not wishing to frighten

Kate with the rioting emotions tumbling through him at her words.

He would be rid of her? He ground his teeth, detesting the idea immediately. Not to mention that her brother and brother-in-law were paying for debt that was not theirs to bear. "If you wish to be rid of this agreement by including your family, I shall forgive the debt. It was wrong of me in the first place to allow such an agreement for us to pass. I should have done the right thing and let what was owed go. I apologize, Lady Brassel." Hearing that Astoridge and Orford would know what he had allowed sent a bolt of panic through him. Would they force him into marriage? He swallowed the terror at having a choice made for him, not his own doing. He enjoyed Kate and their time together, but marriage?

She watched him, her face paling at his words. "They will not know what we have been doing, Your Grace. They will only know of the debt, but that does not mean we cannot be friends. That we may continue what we have started?"

Was she trying to trap him into marriage? Continue the affair until caught and forced to exchange vows? What game was Kate playing, asking him to continue their rendezvous when there was no reason for them to?

"There is no need for us to come together any longer, Lady Brassel. Now, let me escort you inside, and I shall wish you a pleasant evening."

Her smile faltered, but she nodded, allowing him to pull her toward the terrace.

"I would like to say, however," he continued. "That I have enjoyed our time together. I do wish you every happiness, and in future, I hope we shall meet as friends."

"As friends?" she repeated, her tone but a whisper. "Yes,

of course, Your Grace," she said, clearing her voice. "Good evening to you, and I wish you well on your journey north."

Wolfe watched her slip free of his grip and walk away. Head held high and back ramrod straight. Did she mean what she said? Did he?

Damn it all to hell. What was he doing? What was she up to?

He ran a hand through his hair, discombobulated and unsure of his next move.

A feeling of loss assaulted him for the first time, and he was unsure how to remove it.

You do not want a wife, remember?

No, he did not, so why did he feel as if he had allowed an opportunity, a woman he cared for, more than he ought, to slip out of his fingers?

What if she married another? What if she was lost to him again?

He cringed, uncertain what to do, think, or feel before turning on his heel and making a hasty exit. That, at least, was a sound decision, if only the first he'd made in the past few weeks.

K ate swallowed the lump in her throat and worked her way around the outer perimeters of the ballroom, determined to make the foyer and return home. She could not stay at the ball. Did not want to see who the duke turned his attention to now that he was free of her.

She had hoped he would do as her sister thought. Turn to her, declare himself committed to continuing their rendezvous, even if money would soon settle the debt owed.

But he had not.

He had bid her adieu and escorted her back inside as if the few weeks they had spent together meant nothing.

Pain clutched her heart, and she took a calming breath, not wishing the tears blurring her vision to slip down her cheeks. The *ton* did not need to know she was upset, and should they see her as she was, on the verge of crying, they would be relentless until they found out what had displeased her.

"The Brassel carriage, thank you," she ordered the footman in the foyer.

For several minutes, she waited, thankfully alone. A footman fetched her cloak, and soon, her carriage was rumbling over the cobbled streets back to her townhouse on Berkley Square.

How was she to endure the picnic at Richmond tomorrow? To be surrounded by friends and Montague. Would he be escorting Lady Jacobs again? She supposed there was no impediment for them to be intimate now.

Her stomach churned, and she swallowed hard. Not to mention, he would be leaving soon, and she did not know when she would see the duke next.

Possibly not for months. Years perhaps?

Kate swiped at her cheek as a runaway tear escaped. She ought not to be crying. He had agreed to an arrangement of her own doing. She was free of him, able to continue her widowhood without being beholden to any man.

And that was the contention.

She did not want to be alone, not after enjoying the many days in Montague's arms. She had relished being his lover, whether under obligation or not. As degrading as that admission was, it was the truth.

And now it was through.

It was no wonder the ladies who had fallen under Montague's spell in the past pined for the man when their liaison was over. And now, so too would she. A fleeting moment of joy and pleasure that she would not have again.

He certainly did not seem to want to continue as she had hoped.

Well, she would have to pull her countenance together by tomorrow morning and face whatever trials the duke would bestow at the picnic.

And she could be friends with him. Enjoy his company and ignore the rumors, the salacious gossip of his latest antics. She had in the past, and she could do so again.

Her sexual appetites did not rule her and she would not allow the duke to hold that power over her. Not when he was no longer interested in being with her that way.

The carriage rolled to a halt, and without waiting for the footman, she opened the carriage door and started up the stairs. As she made the door, the footman opened it, and she entered, heading straight to her rooms.

"Is everything prepared for tomorrow?" she asked, ascending the stairs.

"Yes, my lady. All will be ready by nine. Would you like your maid to accompany you?" the footman asked.

"No, I have family attending and will not require a chaperone." Kate made it upstairs and to her room, locking the door before anyone could see her upset.

She would face tomorrow, and all would be well. She would not allow the duke to see that she was devastated by his choice to stop their affair. The duke was used to women falling ravaged around his buckskin boots. She would not be one of them.

No matter if here and now, her heart ached at the loss of an opportunity that could have been wonderful for them both.

CHAPTER
TWENTY-ONE

Wolfe sat on a chair under a large oak tree and sipped his wine, watching his guests enjoy the picnic he was hosting. Earlier in the day, his servants had traveled down to Richmond, erecting several tables and chairs, linen tablecloths, and an assortment of food. It was only fitting as host and as one of the wealthiest men in London that his picnic was not soon forgotten by those invited.

He leaned back in his chair, listening to the hum of conversation around him. Lady Jacobs sat at his side, speaking to the Duchess Blackhaven regarding Lord Perkins and his wife, who had fled to Scotland with her footman, leaving his lordship quite alone to do as he pleased with his many lovers and notably lesser morals.

He ought not to be listening in on the conversation, and he was surprised that ladies spoke of such things when they believed they were being quiet enough not to be heard, but alas, he was wrong.

He was wrong about a lot of things.

One of his worst errors of judgment walked a path with Lord Saville. A man he could not fault Kate for wanting to spend time with. Should he have a daughter, the viscount was undoubtedly a gentleman he would deem suitable. A capable, level-headed man and not one to whore about.

Unlike himself, who many women of London thought to bed. A conclusion to his liaisons that had suited him.

Until now...

Up until he had met and was intimate with Kate.

Now, he was uncertain who and what he was, what he wanted.

He ran a hand over his jaw, forcing himself to remain in his seat when Lord Saville adjusted Kate's bonnet to ensure the sun did not reach her eyes.

The thought of her marrying Lord Saville, or anyone for that matter, did not sit right. The idea was wrong somehow and wasn't to be borne.

He was a bastard. He did not want her, and nor did he want anyone else to have her.

"Good afternoon, Your Grace."

He turned to find Lady Orford sitting beside him, busily pouring herself tea. When had she sat down? Was he so preoccupied with Kate that he had not noticed?

"Lady Orford. A pleasure as always."

She scoffed, so alike to her sister's forward manners, and he reveled a little at having a piece of Kate beside him for a time. "Did you have an enjoyable ride out to the park?" he asked, ignoring her jibe.

"Yes, very much. Our carriage was most cheerful. We brought Lord Saville and Kate, and we made a merry party of four. Orford, of course, being the other in the carriage, and yet I think he had disappeared down toward the ponds."

"Of course." Wolfe did not say more, but he was sure that Lady Orford coming to sit beside him did have an ulterior motive.

"Orford and my brother Lord Astoridge will call on you tomorrow if it suits to finalize Brassel's debts. We apologize for his lordship's lack of accounting but rest assured, my sister will no longer be in your debt by Friday as discussed."

He took a calming breath. He had played the bastard, allowing her to use her body to pay off a debt. He should not have, and from the cold glance Lady Orford bestowed on him at her words, she thought him lower than the pond scum that sat at the base of the Serpentine.

"Very good," he replied, unwilling to say more. Not entirely certain it would be safe to do so.

"I hear that you'll be soon traveling to Scotland. May I ask when that is to occur?"

He ground his teeth. Did Lady Orford wish to be rid of him? Was she so appalled by his character and what he had allowed that she wanted to see him go as soon as it may be?

His attention moved past the Marchioness to Kate walking with Lord Saville, and he decided that maybe it was best he left sooner rather than later. Without him in town, Kate may circulate more freely, not feeling as though he watched her every move, which he had taken a liking to these past weeks.

"I'll be closing up the townhouse on Grosvenor Square and leaving by Monday at the latest. If that is soon enough to please you, my lady." Wolfe could not help the cutting tone of his words. Being chastised by Lady Orford was like being scolded by Kate. He did not appreciate the sentiment or enjoy how they thought so lowly of him.

You're a rake. Who cares what these tonnish fobs think?

He inwardly swore. It would seem that he cared more than he liked to admit.

"If it pleases you, Lady Brassel, may I call on you?" Lord Saville asked her, holding out his arm.

Kate did not know how to reply. Should she allow him to call? She liked him, of course. He was a pleasant gentleman, but that was as far as her affections went. But nor could she be rude. That was not her nature. "I have not had an at-home since Lord Brassel's death, my lord. But when I do, you'll be sure to receive an invitation."

He smiled, but she could see her answer disappointed him. Kate linked her arm with his and allowed him to lead them back toward the tables and chairs of their picnic. Before she could tell him differently, Lord Saville held out a seat across from Montague and waited for her to sit before seating himself.

She adjusted her seat, looking everywhere but at the duke, whose stern regard was focused solely on her. Was he displeased? Was he annoyed that she had accepted his invitation?

She had done so before they had parted ways and ended their agreement. Perhaps he thought she would not attend? Perhaps she should not have.

Her stomach fluttered uncomfortably, and she gestured to a footman for wine before taking a much-needed sip.

Kate looked to Anwen, and thankfully, her sister noted her unease and pulled Lord Saville into conversation. Montague, blast the man, continued to stare at her, to the point that she could no longer look away.

She lifted her eyes and met his across the table, but if it

were loathing, annoyance she thought to find there, she did not.

But what was this look he was giving her? "Do I have a butterfly on my nose, Your Grace?" she asked, hoping he would look elsewhere and stop making her feel the many emotions that he always lighted within her.

He was maddening and tempting at once, and he was no longer hers to toy with. To enjoy and sneak away with whenever it pleased them.

He stood and came and sat closer, so much so that they were quite the cozy pair at the table. "Did you have a pleasant stroll with Lord Saville? Are we to expect an announcement soon? He is certainly a gentleman that one ought to marry."

She glared at him, unable to fathom that he would ask such a question. "I beg your pardon, Your Grace, but I fail to see why you should care what my future holds. You've made it perfectly clear that you have no interest in my welfare."

"That is not entirely true," he returned, a muscle working in his temple. "Just because we no longer have an arrangement, I thought... I hoped we would be friends."

Kate fought not to scoff at his words. Friends indeed. She could no sooner be friends with the man than she could a wolf. Both were exceedingly sneaky and prone to bite when provoked.

The duke's bite is delicious, remember...

Kate ignored her wayward thought and schooled her features to one of indifference. "Friends between the sexes is difficult, and for us to speak so intimately would be challenging, I believe, and not advisable."

"In any case, should you look to marry again, know that I approve of Lord Saville. He would be a good husband."

"I had a good husband." She met his eyes, wanting to rail at him that she did not want another benign, happy medium in her life. She wanted fire and passion, life to the fullest, and a man who sparked all those emotions.

Like the man speaking to her now. If only he would stop being obstinate and see what was before him. A woman who adored him, no matter his many faults and wicked past, a woman willing to overlook all those things for a chance to win his heart.

"And he would be a good husband, too."

"Is that what you wish to say to me, Your Grace? We're now on such familiar terms that you want to advise me on who I ought to marry?" Kate could not hold back the derision from her words. "How dare you. How dare you even speak to me after everything we have done and..."

"A walk, if you please, Lady Brassel." The duke held out his arm, and she looked at it before wrapping her arm about his and letting him lead her away from the table.

As soon as they were away from hearing, she rounded on him. "You do not get to tell me who would suit me. I shall choose whom I marry. If I marry at all, which right now I have no plans. You may be able to walk away without a backward glance, and perhaps it is a failure of my sex that we find such situations difficult, but our time together was infuriating as much as it was exciting, and I apologize if I cannot merely shift to someone new so well as you."

He glanced at her, and her stomach churned, making her regret the last glass of champagne she all but downed in one sip.

"I hope you have not grown feelings toward me, my lady," he said, his face turning to stone.

Kate winced as her stomach rejected his words and everything she had consumed since arriving in the park.

Without warning, she hunched and cast up her accounts. The last humiliation for the day, for her life as she knew it, seeing the Duke of Montague's shiny Hessian boots splatter with vomit.

Dear Lord, if only she could die right now. That, at least, would be a future she'd agree to.

CHAPTER
TWENTY-TWO

"Kate!" Wolfe exclaimed before he thought better of using her given name aloud and in front of many influential players in the *ton*. He reached for her as her stomach yielded another violent outburst that he'd never thought possible from the fairer sex.

"All is well," he heard Lady Orford state, seeing her out of his peripheral vision hastily approaching them.

He took Kate's hand and led her over toward a shady area of the park. She leaned against a tree, her face pale, her skin marred with a light sheen of sweat.

"What is wrong?" he asked. "Do you think it was something you ate?"

She shook her head, holding her stomach as if it still pained her. "No, well...I do not know. I felt well this morning, but now I do not feel myself. I should return home."

"Let me escort you," he suggested. "My carriage is large and comfortable, and if Lady Orford," he said, turning to Kate's sister, "will escort Lady Jacobs in return, that would be most helpful. If Lady Brassel suffers from a contagious ague, I think it best that she does not socialize any more than she already has."

Lady Orford threw him a dubious glance but relented to his suggestion. "Very well, that will be best under the circumstances. I shall ensure Lady Jacobs returns to London. But I do think you ought to leave now, Your Grace. My sister does not look at all well."

"I agree." He took Kate's arm and led her toward his carriage. His driver opened the door, always ready for his master, lowering the steps for them both. "London, Phillips, and if I knock on the roof, pull over immediately. Lady Brassel is poorly."

"Of course, Your Grace," his driver agreed.

Within minutes, they were ensconced in the carriage and on their way toward the city. The road was thankfully well traveled, and this part of the journey was not too uneven and uncomfortable.

Even so, with each roll of the wheel, Wolfe noted, Kate's complexion varied from gray to green. "Should I call for a doctor upon our return?" he asked, his concern growing with each minute. Would she be well? Was this more serious than they all first thought?

"It'll pass, I'm certain," she mumbled before clutching her stomach again.

Several times, they stopped and started, barely making hedge way out of the park until Kate lay limp and restless on the squabs, her body overwhelmed by her ailment.

Wolfe leaned out the window to be heard better by the driver. "Divert to Hill Lodge. Lady Brassell is too unwell to travel further. We must halt."

"Of course, Your Grace," his driver said.

It did not take long before the carriage turned into the small manor house. A haven for Kate, who seemed far from well. The housekeeper came out of the inn, the ducal coat of arms on the carriage door no doubt announcing his arrival before he could introduce himself.

"Your Grace," the elderly woman said, bowing. "Is there something I may assist you with?"

"I must fall at Countess Pembroke's feet and ask if we may stay here this evening. We were picnicking in the park, and Lady Brassel has fallen ill."

"Oh, well, Lady Pembroke is not here, Your Grace. She is in London, but I'm certain her ladyship would not turn you away. Do, please, come inside, and I shall have a room prepared for you both."

"Thank you."

"Of course." The housekeeper barked out orders and aided Kate upstairs. The house was busy, considering Lady Pembroke was not in residence. Thankfully, upstairs was more subdued, and they were soon led into a large room, multiple maids fixing the bed and pulling window dressings open to the daylight. Others lit the fire and prepared the bath.

Wolfe helped Kate over to a chair near the hearth. "We require a bucket. I apologize, but Lady Brassel is quite unwell, as you can see."

Within minutes, their every desire was met, and thankfully, the bath was filled.

"I do not know what is wrong with me. Do you think it was something I ate, or I have caught something dreadful from someone?" She looked to him for guidance.

He kneeled beside her chair and, without thought, pushed her dark locks, long fallen out of her fashionable coiffure, from her face. "I do not know. I have never seen anyone become so ill so quickly before."

"Can you send word that I shall not be home this

evening? My son's nurse will worry, and my staff, if I do not arrive home when I advised them I would."

"Of course," he said, kissing her brow. He stood and moved over to a small desk beside a window. "I shall write a missive now and send it immediately."

"I'm sorry to be a bother, Wolfe," she whispered before another bout of sickness took over her.

He abandoned his letter and went to her, holding back her hair as she retched all that was in her stomach. "It is nothing. There is nowhere else I would rather be."

Never more accurate words from his mouth.

The duke left her with a maid, and Kate took the opportunity to relieve herself before slipping into the warm bath. She was thankful her gown was removed, allowing her clammy skin to breathe for the first time in hours.

Never had she ever felt so wretched. She sank into the water, wetting her hair and washing her face. The maid passed her a glass of mint water, and she washed out her mouth.

"Thank you," she said before the maid dipped into a curtsy. "Of course, Lady Brassel. I will return downstairs. Do ring the bell should you need anything else."

A light knock sounded on the door several minutes later, along with the muffled tone of Wolfe as he asked to come in. She bid the duke enter. What did it matter if he saw her as she was? It was not as if they had not seen each other before. They had been far more intimate than anyone would guess.

He entered, and she heard him snick the lock on the

door. "I have a tray of food and beverages. Nothing too heavy, but this food will keep if you're hungry later."

"Thank you," she said, leaning back in the tub and closing her eyes. "I do not know how to thank you enough for today. I'm sorry for being trouble. I know you escorted Lady Jacobs, and I probably spoiled your plans with her ladyship this evening."

Kate peeked at the duke, wanting him to dismiss her words, tell her that she was wrong, that she had interrupted his designs on the woman, but he did not.

Instead, he shrugged and went about the room, removing his coat and waistcoat before laying them over a nearby chair.

He loosened his cravat and rolled up his sleeves. "Let me wash your hair. I believe you may have been sick in it today."

Kate cringed and leaned forward to allow him access to her long locks.

The duke pulled a small stool up against the tub and picked up a nearby cake of soap. He rubbed it into her hair, massaging her skull with an ability that left her drowsy and far too aware of his presence than she needed right at this moment.

You're ill, Kate. You're not supposed to be having inappropriate thoughts about the duke!

And yet she was. She could not help herself. Somewhere in her absurd plan to pay off a debt, she had fallen for the rake, and there was no getting over that in a day or so.

"You're very good at washing hair. Perhaps you ought to take up the occupation full-time."

He chuckled, the deep timbre of his voice making her skin prickle in awareness. "I only wash the hair of exceptional people, and you are one of those. For all that has happened between us, Kate, I do care for you. I'm not without feelings, even though I believe you think I'm heartless and cold."

She turned to him, and he grinned. "I hope you are not," she said, tipping her head to the side when his grin became a short chuckle. "What is so amusing? What are you laughing at?"

"You have an abundance of soap in your hair. In fact, you look like you're wearing a Georgian wig. Best to lie back in the bath and rinse it if you can."

She smiled and dipped into the water, doing as he suggested. She rinsed her hair quickly before coming back up. "Is that better?" she asked.

He cleared his throat and nodded. "Yes, much better."

Kate met his gaze and saw the hunger burning in his blue eyes. She wanted to throw herself into his arms, into the promise of ecstasy his hold vowed, but she could not.

Not only because she was unwell, but because, for all his care this afternoon, there was no future with His Grace. He was a bachelor, a man determined to remain alone forever, and she would not be the lady to change his mind.

For a moment, she had hoped she would be, but desire, lust even, was not enough to build a relationship, a marriage upon. She wanted her next husband, if she decided to marry, to love, adore, make love to her, and live a full and happy life.

Not marry a man who would regret his decision within days of saying "I do".

The duke reached for a nearby drying cloth. "Here, come, I shall help you out and to dress. Your shift will have to do this evening, I'm afraid. You need sleep, and when you are well again, I shall take you back to London."

She nodded and stood, the water sloshing onto the floor

and the duke's Hessian boots. "Oh dear, I do not think your boots will survive me this day," she teased, making light of their situation.

The duke's gaze raked her from head to toe, his mouth opening on a gasp. "Well, if my shoes do not survive, neither will my heart, for dear God, Kate. You are a beautiful woman."

She stepped out of the bath and wrapped herself with the towel he held. "Thank you, but you're right. I need to sleep. I feel terribly tired all of a sudden."

He mumbled something under his breath that she could not decipher, and maybe it was best she could not. She had more pressing concerns, namely keeping from casting up her accounts and making herself more of a nuisance than she already was.

CHAPTER
TWENTY-THREE

K ate woke in a tangle of arms and legs. The warm, familiar body at her side comforted her, and she dared not move for several minutes, wanting to revel in the feel of Wolfe in her arms once again.

She took a deep, relieved breath that her stomach no longer seized with pain, and she felt more herself, merely a little more fatigued than usual. But that was any wonder after the ordeal she just endured.

Kate wiggled out of his hold and rinsed her mouth again with a glass of mint water beside her bed. Thankfully, the staff did not seem to care the duke remained in her room, and with her so sick, should it come out in London, hopefully, the excuse would suffice.

Not that a part of her hoped his concern, his being here, looking after her, wasn't due to his feeling something more than mere friendship.

She snuck back into bed and reached for him. He turned to her, snuggling into her side, his lips brushing her shoulder. Kate ran her hand through his hair, staring at the ceiling, and debated what to do.

The urge to cry into the dark that she loved him and would he please love her back almost gained the better of her senses.

His touch on her skin intensified, and he kissed his way up her neck, tickling the underside of her ear and making her squirm.

"Are you feeling better?" he asked, his hand sliding along one side of her waist.

She wanted to feel his touch. Her body, without thought, reached for him in return. "I am, thank you. You have been such an aid today. I do not think I would have survived back to London had you not called in at Hill Lodge."

"I would say it was my pleasure, but I take no delight from seeing you so unwell. I'm glad you're much improved."

"I am." They stared at each other for several heartbeats before he brushed his lips against hers.

Kate reached for him, having missed him these past few days. She kissed him back, deepened the embrace, and told him without words that she wanted and needed him more than anything.

He returned her ardor, his tongue taunting hers. They came together, their bodies wrapping about each other. Wolfe gathered her shift, settling between her legs, and then they were one.

Kate gasped when he thrust into her. She wrapped her legs around his waist, but the joining was different. It was not as fast or demanding as it often had been. This time, it was slow, a dance of desire that left her heart pumping fast and her mind reeling with possibility.

She met Wolfe's eyes, his heavy with desire. This was no quick tupping, a fleeting passionate moment, oh no.

The Wild Wolfe of London was making love to her...

Her stomach dipped with pleasure, and she cradled his face, pulling him down for another kiss. She held on to him, never wanting this moment to end. How would she survive without the touch of this man? Without seeing him every day. To jest, to try her every nerve. What was life if it were filled with only mediocre nothings?

"Kate," he groaned.

She knew the madness that was rushing through his veins, hers was the same. "Wolfe, I..." How she wanted to declare herself, to tell him all that he made her feel.

I love you, she whispered in her mind.

"You undo me. I..." He pulled her closer still, his arms like a vise, and with one last thrust, she shattered in his embrace. Pleasure spiked through her body, curling through her.

She groaned, called his name, and kissed him deep and long as he, too, found his release. No, this was no use. She could not go on like this. They could not keep pretending nothing was happening between them.

Because it was.

Wolfe pulled her into the crook of his arm. They caught their breath for several minutes and fought to calm their racing hearts. He stared down at her, and she came up to lean atop his chest, needing to watch him as she took a leap of faith and did what she must.

Be honest with him.

"Wolfe," she began, fighting the nerves that told her to be quiet, to let him go, to continue on as they agreed. "I need to tell you something, and I need you to listen to me before replying. Will you do that for me?" she asked.

A small frown formed between his brows, but he

nodded. "Of course, if you wish, but you do have me curious."

She smiled and hoped her words only made him curious, and did not cause him to bolt for the door and away from her before she finished stating them. "Wolfe," she said, knowing it was now or never. "I've fallen in love with you."

He stilled beneath her, and for several beats of her racing heart, he did not respond. What was he thinking? She wished she knew.

"Is that all you wished to say?" he asked.

He moved out from beneath her, hunching over the side of the bed before standing and moving toward where his clothes lay over a nearby chair.

"You cannot love me. I do not need your love."

Kate rolled her eyes and leaned against the bed head. She crossed her arms over her chest, wishing he would look at her when they spoke. "I know you do not need my love, but I have fallen in love with you anyway. I want a future with you, and I think you want one with me, deep down in your guarded heart."

"Well, I'm sorry I'll disappoint you."

"Stop, Wolfe. Look at me and tell me you do not feel that there is something more between us." She gestured to the bed. "Like just before, for instance. You cannot make love to someone so tenderly, so sweetly, and not feel any emotion at all. I know you care for me, and I think you're struggling with who you were and may someday be. I love both versions of you, you see. Your past and your future, and I want to be the lady who becomes the next Duchess of Montague."

He turned to her then, and she could see he struggled with everything she said. Did he believe her? Did he suspect she may be right? No doubt all those emotions were coiling through him now, but how would he react? What would he say and do? That was the question.

"I do not want a wife. You knew this when entering the agreement that you desired. I have a mistress, a comfortable life, and no ties. Nor do I want any, and marrying you or anyone would pin me down and limit my life in ways I will not allow. So no, I do not want to marry you. I do not love you, and I'm sorry you believed otherwise. I do like you, Kate. But you will only ever be my friend's widowed wife. There will be nothing more between us."

Kate threw back the bedding and stormed over to him. "I call bollocks on that. You're a liar, Your Grace. You do care for me. I feel it every time we're alone. With each touch and kiss, you give yourself away. Perhaps you ought to admit that I'm right and you're wrong and that you do love me and that you wish to marry me."

He crossed his arms, staring down at her as if she had lost her mind, and maybe she had a little. But she could no longer stand by, be intimate, give her heart and body to this man, and not admit to what she was feeling, how she loved him.

Even the vexing side of him that refused to budge or agree to her words.

"I do that with all my lovers."

His words, damn them, prickled her heart, but she would not relent.

Don't give up on him without a fight.

"So you care for all your lovers when they're ill as I was today. You hold all their hair back so they do not make a mess within it. You help them bathe and everything else you did for me?"

A muscle worked in his jaw, and he glanced toward the

door, the bed, the ceiling, anywhere but her face. "Of course."

Kate stepped back, shaking her head. "Very well, Your Grace. Have it your way, but now I see the shield you're placing between us, and I'm sorry for you for needing this barrier. You do love me. You may not know it right now, hell, you may not even wish to admit to it, which you do not, but you do love me. I only hope that you come to your senses before it is too late."

"And what does that mean?" he asked, taking a step toward her. "Are you considering another proposal? Did Lord Saville disclose his intentions to you today?"

"He asked to call on me, yes, and I have not said I would not admit him should he drop in at Berkley Square," she lied, omitting the part where she agreed he could call so long as it was during an at-home.

The duke thought about her words before he shrugged and started pulling on his waistcoat over his shirt. "You may do as you please. We may have been lovers, but that does not mean you cannot take another now that I'm leaving."

"When are you leaving?" she asked, unable to hide the tremor of panic from her voice.

"Monday, I leave for Scotland. I will not return before the next Season or the following year. I'm still determining. But I'll be sure to return if I receive an invitation to your wedding with the viscount."

Kate bit the inside of her lip, willing herself not to cry. He did not need to see her upset. There would be plenty of time for that when she returned home. "Please go downstairs and fetch a maid. I wish to dress and return to London. You may go. I shall take loan of one of Lady

Pembroke's carriages to return to Mayfair. I do not think it is wise for us to be alone anymore."

"Do not be hysterical, Lady Brassel. I shall escort you home as I promised. But I shall leave you now to dress and see you downstairs."

Kate stared at the shuttered window, hearing the duke ring for a maid before exiting the room and, with it, all her hopes of a future with him.

CHAPTER
TWENTY-FOUR

The ride back to London was uncomfortable at best and disastrous at worst. Kate sat silent and focused on anything that moved past the carriage window, refusing to look at him.

She loved him?

Her declaration bashed about in his mind like a drum and would not relent. He'd never expected her to disclose how she felt. While he may have wondered a time or two if she were growing feelings for him, he had not thought they would be as strong as love.

Love?

Dear Lord in heaven, he'd never loved a woman apart from his mama. He could not love Kate in return. He would only end up hurting her, possibly even more than she was disappointed with Brassel.

He was rotten to his core, a rake, a man used to getting his way and women falling at his feet. Selfish and impulsive. To remain chaste and never sleep with another woman again was as foreign to him as speaking Greek.

No, she would be much better off falling out of love

with him and finding another to marry—a man who wished for the commitment to begin with and one who loved her in return.

The thought made him want to punch the carriage's wall, but that did not mean he loved her. Cared, certainly. They were friends. Had for several weeks enjoyed each other's company immensely.

But love?

No. That was out of the question.

"Are you ever going to speak to me again?" he asked. "Your feelings will ease, and soon you will find a gentleman who will make your heart beat for him only. I'm certain of it."

Slowly, she turned her head to meet his gaze. Her features oozed loathing, so much so he could not quite believe what he was looking at. Was she indeed so angry at him?

"Do not mock me, Your Grace. Do not spew your condescending words to me, now or ever. I know what I feel. Why I feel the way I do about you is a mystery to me right now, but I'm certain when I've calmed down, I shall remember what makes me love you. But do not dismiss my feelings so easily. You may not want to hear them, but for me, they are true and as real as I'm sitting here."

Her words shamed him. He never wanted to make her feel as though he mocked her. "I only mean to make the hurt you're feeling right now a little less if that is possible." Wolfe reached for her, and she slapped his hand away.

"Only time will heal my heart, and I apologize, Your Grace, if I have not done so as quickly as you'd like. It has been but an hour since we left Hill Lodge. I may need two."

Wolfe ignored her barb, and thankfully, the carriage rumbled to a halt before her townhouse. A footman opened the door, lowering the steps. He went to alight to assist her, but she waved him away.

"I do not need your service. God forbid the Duke of Montague be needed by a lady. How terrifying that thought must be to you." She stepped onto the footpath, slamming the door and meeting his eye through the window. "I wish you well, Montague. I hope you enjoy your Highlands and your whores."

Wolfe watched her turn on her heel and leave without a backward glance. He ran a hand through his hair as Kate disappeared into her townhouse.

He banged on the carriage roof, and relief swamped him when they were out of sight of the house. This is what he wanted. What he needed to do to be happy.

Are you certain?

Of course, it was. He knew no other way of life. He was free to do as he pleased, make love to anyone he wished, travel, and be beholden to no one.

But then that also meant that Kate was free to do the same. Would she take a lover but remain unmarried? Would he hear rumors at Whites of the lucky bastard whom she allowed such liberties with?

Even now, his hands fisted at his sides, and the thought of pummelling the bastard to a pulp came to mind.

When he was in Scotland, all would be well. Once she was out of his system and he was free from seeing her, his rendezvous with Lady Kate Brassel would be nothing but a pleasant memory and one he was determined to leave in the past.

. . .

K ate stood in the library and watched as Montague's carriage turned around the corner on Berkeley Square and out of sight.

She rang for a servant and waited, watching children play in the park across the street.

"You called, Lady Brassel?" John asked from the doorway.

"Yes," she said, turning to her servant. "I'd like to leave for Brassel Estate tomorrow. The servants can close the house and travel to Kent when everything is as it should be here."

"Would you like Mr. Freedman to remain to care for the gardens and keep a watch on the house?"

She thought about it momentarily and knew that Mr. Freedman had a family in town. This was what he would prefer in any case. "That would be best, I think. Please inform the staff and have my maid pack my things and Oliver's as well."

"Of course, my lady."

The last two days had been taxing. Her body craved rest, the need to sleep, making her eyes heavy. She walked over to the settee and sat, staring at the unlit hearth.

He rejected her?

Even now, she could not quite believe that was so. She had thought he would have declared his undying love to her. Offer marriage, and they would have ridden off into the sunset...

Well, perhaps not as romantic as that, but she had not expected him to repudiate her so harshly. His words were as cold as if he had never had a glimmer of emotional attachment to her at all.

The sound of the front door opening and closing ignited

a spark of hope that Montague had seen the error of his ways, but it was not to be. Her sister stormed into the library and sighed in relief at the sight of her.

"You're back. I was worried sick. Your maid sent word to me last evening that you were staying at Hill Lodge. Were you so sick that you needed respite there?" she asked, sitting beside her and taking her hand.

"I do not think I've ever been more ill in my life. Montague was very supportive, but..." The lump, the tears she had held at bay, broke free, and her sister swam in her vision.

"Kate, what is wrong?" Anwen asked, her tone one of apprehension.

"I'm a fool. I declared my feelings to the duke, and he rejected me. He does not love me. Said so to my face. I will never live down the shame."

"There is no shame in being honest with yourself and others." Anwen pulled her into an embrace. "There, there, all will be well. He will right his wrong, I'm certain of it. No one who has been in the duke's company would believe he does not love you. If he is deceiving anyone, it's himself."

Her sister's words brought comfort, but there was little she could do unless Montague actioned her sister's thoughts. And she certainly could not live in hope, wait around for the duke to know his own mind.

Worse still, her sister could be wrong, and the duke was telling the truth.

He does not love me.

"Well, I shall not be waiting around to find out. I'm going to travel to Kent tomorrow. Return home for a year or two. I don't know if I shall return next Season. Little Olivar is so young, and it will be all too soon before he leaves for Eton. I do not wish to miss any of his milestones."

"You are not staying for the remainder of the Season? I shall miss seeing you," Anwen said, her face one of compassion, but understanding.

"I will miss you too, but this is for the best. I do not wish to see the duke continue his bachelorhood or hear any rumors about town of his antics. Not now that I have feelings toward the rogue, he is to travel to Scotland, but even from up there, he is a man everyone discusses and gossips about. I do not want to be here to hear any of it."

Her sister nodded. "I understand, and I shall ensure Orford and I come and see you before Christmas. We shall have a jolly party. I shall bring the children too."

"Dom and Paris could also attend. I would love to have you all with me for a time."

"That sounds perfect." Anwen stood and rang the bellpull. "I think tea is in order."

"A wonderful idea." Kate was quite parched, and her stomach was unsettled after the carriage ride.

"Were you so very ill yesterday?"

"Oh, Anwen, it was horrendous. The housekeeper at Hill Lodge allowed us to stay, and the duke said he would apologize and thank Lady Pembroke for her staff's trouble. But it was unlike anything I've ever known and so very sudden. Even now, I'm not feeling the best. I do believe it was the fish cakes that I ate. Perhaps they had sat in the sun too long."

"It could be, but I ate two of those myself, and I feel fine." Anwen pursed her lips. "You have been stressed, and Montague is the cause of that tension most of all. It was no wonder you were ill. He probably gave you an ulcer."

Kate chuckled and thanked a maid who brought in a steaming pot of tea and two cups. "Well, I shall be rid of him, and with any luck, I will soon be over my foolish love for the man. He believes it will only take me a short while to move on and forget him." Kate shook her head, unable to fathom how stupid some men were. "I fear his denial of me means we have missed a wonderful opportunity for happiness, Anwen. One that I do not think I shall ever feel with anyone ever again."

Anwen nodded, the frown between her brows deepening. "Well, he is foolish then, and it serves him right when, years from now, he is a lonely old man full of regrets. Let us see if his whores keep him warm then."

CHAPTER
TWENTY-FIVE

Three weeks later, Kent

Kate sat outside on the lawns, laughing as little Oliver ran about her with his small Pomeranian and nanny who chased him in turn. His happy squeal of delight that escaped him every now and then, bringing her comfort. Pleasure filled her at watching her small boy, his cheerful countenance and exuberance for life making her wish she had more of the same.

She clutched her stomach, holding the second life growing inside her, and not for the first time, wondering what she would do. How would she free herself of the mess she had made?

Not that she could regret the baby who was coming. If she could, she would remain in Kent for the rest of her life, bring up her children, and be happy to allow the *ton* to gossip and shun her.

But she could not do that to the children. She needed to marry to protect them and ensure no scandal ever shadowed their doors, not of her doing in any case.

The thought made her want to cast up her accounts. How could she marry another man when her heart beat for Montague?

He, of course, would be well on his way to Scotland by now. Her sister wrote and informed her he had left town as planned. Not that she had heard a word from him, and considering he wished for them to be friends, Kate could not help but be hurt a little by his ability to forget her so quickly.

"Mama, a flower for you."

Kate took the small, violet bonnet-shaped Columbine blossom. "Thank you, my darling boy. It is beautiful."

He smiled and ran off to his nanny again, and Kate watched as they linked hands and started toward the house. Oliver was due for his afternoon nap, and no doubt Nanny needed a little respite after all that running about.

"Kate!"

She turned at her sister's voice and waved. Her sister joined her on the lawn, sitting beside her and bussing her cheek. "Oh, how delightful it is to be out of the carriage. I'm so happy we're here."

"As am I. Are Dom and Paris with you?" she asked.

"They are, but Paris wanted to go upstairs and change. The roads were surprisingly dusty for this time of year, but I wanted to see you first."

Kate smiled and, looking up at the sky, shut her eyes. "I have had an offer of marriage from Lord Saville, and I will accept it. I merely have to write him back and give him the good news."

Her sister's silence stretched, and Kate opened one eye to see what she was up to. The horror written across her sister's features would have been comical had it not been because of what she disclosed. "You do not agree, I see."

"Why would you do such an absurd thing? Lord Saville is a kind, good-natured gentleman, but you do not love him and will be as bored as you were with Brassel. I will not allow you to marry another man out of duty."

Kate sighed, lying back on the linen rug she sat upon. "It is time I married. Lord Saville will do as well as anyone else. I think I shall be happy with him. He will make a good father for Oliver, and that is all that matters."

"Your feelings matter also, and you do not know if he will be good with Oliver. Men say and do many things to enable marriage, but it does not always mean they're showing their true selves. What if he is not as he appears?"

Kate did not think Saville was capable of such duplicity. No, he would be well, and that would be that. "He is as he appears. Stop trying to talk me out of it."

Anwen lay down beside her, and Kate met her eyes. "What is going on, sister? You were not looking for a husband in London, and certainly not after Montague. Why the change of heart?"

Kate did not want to explain or want to see her sister lose her equilibrium, but she could not lie to her either. How would she tell a sibling she was pregnant to a man who did not want her?

She did not reply. Anwen watched her keenly, too close for comfort, and Kate saw the moment her sister understood her need for a husband.

"Oh, Kate. I'm so sorry, my darling."

Kate bit her lip, swiping at her cheek as a tear slipped free. "All will be well. I'm early enough that no one will know. If I marry soon and do not delay. I thought to invite Lord Saville here while you are all in attendance. No one can then say a word about the baby when it comes or question my reputation. Not that I'm frightened for myself, but I am for the children. I do not want them to be injured by the situation I now find myself in."

Anwen reached for her hand and clasped it. "Have you thought about writing to Montague and telling him? This type of news may make him think again about his choices, and he may wish to make things right."

Kate shook her head, having already thought endlessly about writing to him. Even going so far as starting numerous letters over the past week, but no. He did not want a wife or the children that arose from having one. He was happy as a bachelor, and there was no reason he ever needed to know that her second child was his.

Guilt prickled at the thought, and she pushed it aside.

Even if she did long for him and wished daily that things could have ended differently, they had not.

"Montague made it clear that he does not love me. What he does not know will not hurt him, Anwen. Promise me always to keep my secret. What I've told you today can never be known by Lord Saville or anyone." The guilt she felt at having to keep such a secret from Saville and Montague ate at her already and she did not know how she would survive it all. But she must. So much, her children's future, her reputation depended on it.

"I promise not to say a word, and I shall help you prepare for a wedding. All will be well, sister. You will see."

Kate could barely smile at the notion. She did not wish to marry anyone she did not love, but what choice did she have? Any woman in her position would do anything to save her family's reputation, and she would also, even if that action meant another mediocre, benign marriage that was as unfulfilling as her last.

CHAPTER
TWENTY-SIX

One week later, somewhere along the Great North Road

The trip to Scotland was the worst mistake of his life. How he thought removing himself from Kate's presence, away from society and the possibility of running into her at balls and parties, was beyond him.

The inability to see her, to call and catch glimpses of her at social events, left him distracted and shamefully more irritable than he liked to think himself.

Wolfe made it as far as Edinburgh before he ordered the carriage around and headed back for London.

His mistress sat across from him, surly and untalkative, and he could not blame her. He'd not wanted her to touch him from the moment they left London, nor did he find her as appealing as he once had.

The woman was bored and possibly exhausted from the travel that led nowhere. Not to mention, she was not Kate.

Damn, he had made a mess of things, and how would he repair the damage? It had taken him three weeks to reach Edinburgh and now another three to return to London.

But return he must. He needed to see Kate. Hear her voice and hold her in his arms. An outcome he'd never thought to require, and yet, the idea of her being so far away from him, living a life without him in it, drove him to distraction.

"I do not know why you brought me with you if you do not wish to use my services. I could have found a new gentleman by now, and you would be free to be the chaste, henpecked husband you wish to be."

Sally's words at one time would have severed him silent and full of unease, but now he could do nothing but agree with her. That is exactly what he wanted to do and be.

"Again, Sally, I apologize for bringing you all this way for no reason, and you'll be sure to be compensated."

She mumbled something under her breath before she pursed her lips, watching him. "Well, I suppose I cannot be too angry then," she hedged, her tone much warmer than it had been just before. "Of course, being your mistress these past years and the woman you shunned will make me the talk of the town. I shall be the last woman to have slept with the Wild Wolfe of London before he became a husband. I'm certain I shall enjoy the notoriety that credential will bring me."

Wolfe laughed. There was little he could say or do, and of course, Sally was right. She was the last woman to share his bed before Kate occupied every facet of his life.

"We shall arrive at the Goldfinch Inn soon and shall change horses. I will hire a room so you may rest and refresh yourself before we start our journey anew."

"May we have luncheon? I'm terribly hungry already."

He nodded. "Of course."

Within half an hour, the carriage turned into the inn's yard and stopped before an old wooden door that had seen many a year. Wolfe alighted and helped Sally down, moving indoors. His steps faltered when he spied Lord Billington partaking in a brew in the taproom.

"Can I help ye, Your Grace?" the innkeeper asked, looking between him and Sally as if he knew who the woman was and what she was hired to do.

Wolfe ignored his salacious smirk. "A room, while the horses are changed for my companion and please send up wine and something to eat. I shall break my fast in the taproom."

"Of course, Your Grace." The innkeeper escorted Sally up the stairs, and Wolfe went to where Billington sat alone enjoying his ale.

"Billington," he said, sitting at the viscount's side.

Billington's eyes went wide before he smiled. "Montague. What are you doing here? I thought you ought to be in Scotland by now."

Wolfe ordered a beer and took a welcome sip before answering, "Yes, you are right, but I changed my mind, and I'm returning to London early. Unfinished business that requires my urgent attention."

The viscount's brow rose in interest. "Well, I hope everything is sorted soon for you."

"I hope so, too," he said. "Tell me, what brings you here? Are you headed to your estate or back to London also?"

"Ah, well, the same, but I'm heading back to London to pick up the countess before heading to Kent. I was at our estate in York, but we have been invited to a wedding, which will take place as soon as we arrive. You know how long mail can take and travel takes time. The countess shall be displeased if she misses her friend's wedding."

The thought that he too would be having a wedding, a summarization that he never thought to imagine warmed his soul. He would ensure everyone they knew was invited to enjoy their happy day.

He could not wait to tell Kate that he was wrong. That in his pigheaded, obstinate ways, he had not been able to recognize that his affection for her was love.

But the farther the miles took him from her, the more he knew he had made a mistake. But he could repair the rift, throw himself at her feet, and beg forgiveness.

"May I ask who is marrying? Perhaps you could send my warmest regards and felicitations if I know the gentleman and lady."

Billington chuckled and stared at him as if he had lost his mind. "The Wild Wolfe of London is wishing a couple very happy? Well, I never thought to see the day." He paused, sipping his beer. "The wedding is between Lord Saville and Lady Brassel. One more bann to call, and they can be married. Everyone is down at the Brassel estate, enjoying the celebrations before dear Kate becomes Lady Saville."

Wolfe stumbled out of his chair, and he fought to breathe as the air in his lungs expelled and would not return. She was engaged? To Saville?

Why? How?

It could not be true. She would not do such a foolish thing.

"Are you well, Montague?" Billington asked, reaching for him.

He waved him away, stumbling toward the door. "I am well. I merely remembered a pressing concern I must reach London for before it is too late," he lied.

Wolfe called the innkeeper and ordered his carriage

ready and Sally to come post haste. He needed to get to Kent as fast as the horses could gallop.

She was getting married?

Damn it all to hell, she would not. Not if he had anything to do about it. The only person she would marry was him, and anyone who thought otherwise could meet him at dawn.

CHAPTER
TWENTY-SEVEN

Tomorrow was her wedding day.

The idea ought to bring joy, and yet, Kate could not help but feel as though she were being unfaithful to Wolfe. At the very least, untruthful to both Wolfe and Lord Saville.

Not that it mattered. She had not seen Montague for six weeks, and he would be in Scotland by now. Even if she were to send word to notify him of their baby, by the time he arrived in Kent, should he wish to save her reputation at all, she would be far too gone in the pregnancy for anyone to believe the baby was conceived in wedlock.

She stood at the window in the conservatory, taking in the view of the slow-flowing river that ran through the estate. The house was full of guests, everyone they knew was here for the wedding, and the house vibrated with excitement and laughter.

And while she smiled and laughed when fitting, whenever she gained a moment's peace, her mask slipped, and she often found herself nervous, reflective, and full of regret.

What have I done?

The dinner gong sounded, and Kate made her way toward the dining room, ignoring the protocol that she should have been in the withdrawing room before dinner to meet with her guests.

She walked into the dining room, hearing a commotion and raised voices, and her steps quickened.

"What is happening in here?" she asked, coming into the room and finding most of the guests seated except Lord Saville and one other.

Montague.

Who stood nose to nose with Saville?

"Kate," he said, striding toward her.

A whispered gasp sounded from the table, and Kate felt all the guests' attention move to her. Out of her peripheral sight, she knew their mouths gaped at what was happening before them.

Which right at this exact time, she wasn't entirely certain herself.

"Your Grace." She remembered to dip into a curtsy. "What brings you to Kent?" she asked, pasting on a smile while her stomach churned with nerves.

"You're getting married? To him?" Wolfe stated, pointing toward Lord Saville as if marrying the viscount was a preposterous idea.

Kate raised her chin, not letting him criticize her choice, especially when he left her with none.

He does not know about the baby...

She thought about that momentarily, and hope ignited in her soul. If Wolfe did not know about the baby, then he was here because—dare she hope—he loved her? That he had seen the error of his ways?

Not that it aided at all, not now. She was getting

married tomorrow. The scandal she had been trying to avoid would be far worse if she ran off with the Wild Wolfe of London on the eve of her wedding.

"Your Grace, please remain calm and follow me if you will. We will continue this conversation in the library."

His mouth pursed into a displeased line, and he strode past her. Kate turned to Lord Saville. "If you'll excuse me a moment, everyone. I shall not be long."

They mumbled their agreement, and she turned on her heel and left. Wolfe rounded on her no sooner had she entered the library and shut the door.

"So you're marrying Saville? What happened to remaining alone for the rest of your life?"

Kate could not hold back the laugh that bubbled up at his nonsensical remark. "Remain alone for the rest of my life? Why, because you wish me to? What if I had fallen in love with Lord Saville? You have been gone six weeks. That is a long time for a lady being courted."

"You do not love him." His eyes narrowed on her as he paced back and forth in front of her desk. "You love me."

Kate swallowed the hope his words rose within her. This was wrong. She could not call off a wedding that was to take place within a matter of hours.

"It is too late for us now. I have agreed to marry his lordship, and I like him very much. I do not think the marriage will be similar to the one with Brassel. I do believe this one will be better."

"The hell it will be because it shall not occur at all. You're not marrying the viscount."

Kate crossed her arms, her temper getting the better of her determination to remain calm. "Is that so, Your Grace? Well then," she continued. "Do tell me whom I can marry if this decision is up to you."

He stopped pacing and faced her. "You will marry me."

Kate bit the inside of her lip, the prickling of tears tingling her nose. "I will not marry you. You do not wish to be a husband, you stated that yourself. What was it you said again?" She tapped her chin in thought. "Ah, that is right, you do not want a wife or to be beholden to anyone."

He took a step toward her, and she moved back, needing to keep her distance from him if she were to remain clear thinking.

"I was wrong, Kate. So wrong." He shook his head and closed the space between them, bending down to kneel before her. He took her hands and held them, beseeched her with his eyes.

Kate took a fortifying breath and tried to stop the trembling in her knees, but she knew he noted her nervousness.

"I want you as my wife. I made a mistake when I denied you your love. I should have known what I felt that day when you disclosed your love. What savaged my soul was my love for you in return. It is true. I do not wish to be beholden to anyone unless that someone is you."

He reached into his coat pocket and pulled out a ring. Kate gasped at the size of the square diamond set in silver. She had never seen a more exquisite jewel or heard such beautiful words.

"I love you," he stated, his eyes welling with tears.

Kate stared at him, unable to grasp that the Wild Wolfe of London was unrestrained and begging for her hand. She stared at him, not wanting to ever move forward from this moment, so perfect, so precious that it was.

"I love you, Kate. Please say I'm not too late to make you mine. I want us to have a life together, to make a family, and be happy. Please do not marry Saville. I do not wish to shoot him on a field at dawn merely to get my way."

"You are too wild for your own good, Wolfe," she stated. "But you've been away for so long. Why are you not in Scotland with your mistress?"

He remained kneeling, and shame crossed his face. "I did not touch her. I promise you. I could not. She tried, of course, but the idea revolted me, and nothing ever happened. Sally was quite displeased with me that I had taken her halfway to Scotland for no reason. I turned around at Edinburgh, and on my way south, I ran into Lord Billington. He was the one who informed me of your impending wedding. I dashed here to ensure I was not too late. I hope that I am not."

"I'm supposed to marry tomorrow. The banns have been called, the contracts signed."

"I'm the Duke of Montague. All of those problems are nothing but an inconvenience, should you wish them to be. Marry me, Kate. Love me as I love you."

Kate threw herself into his arms, holding him tight. His strong arms embraced her and held her for several minutes.

"I'm so sorry, my darling. I'm so sorry for being blind. I've loved you from afar for so many years. I loved you when you married Brassel, and I had to watch and bear witness to his neglect when I only wanted to have you as my own. I've loved you since you offered that ridiculous arrangement in your library, and I have adored you when you declared your affection like the brave woman you are. Please be mine, Kate. Marry me, and have the wonderful life I know we both can have."

Kate nodded, knowing she could not refuse. Not when he offered his love without knowing the secret she held. It made his declaration all the sweeter. "Yes," she whispered against his ear. "Yes, I shall marry you."

They held each other on the floor, both unwilling to

move. She pulled back and met his eyes. "Lord Saville will be displeased."

"I shall pay him off, and my man of business will sort out all the legalities, but we shall return to London tomorrow and marry by special license. The sooner you're the Duchess of Montague, the better."

She grinned, happiness and disbelief making her head swim. "Can this truly be happening? I did not think I'd ever see the day the Wild Wolfe of London was slain."

He threw her a wicked look, and her skin prickled in awareness. "Not slain, merely tamed by a heroine who knew how to soften his beastly heart."

Kate chuckled at his innuendo. "As he knew his way to hers." She cupped his face in her hands. "I've missed you so much. I did not think I'd ever see you again, but there is something that I think you ought to know." She could not marry him, without telling him of the baby. Fear curled in her stomach that he would be displeased she was willing to marry another to save her and the child's reputation, but she pushed it aside. Wolfe loved her. He would understand...

"What is it?" he asked, his hold on her tightening.

"There is no easy way to tell you this and so I'm just going to get to the point." She paused, taking a fortifying breath. "I'm pregnant with your baby, Wolfe. I'm sorry I did not tell you, but you were so adamant to remain unmarried and I could not burden you with this. I did not want you to marry me out of pity and obligation."

"You're having our baby?" He stared at her for what felt like several minutes. His features shifted from a variety of emotions, she did not want to guess as to how many. "You were going to marry Saville to save your reputation and the baby's? Does Saville know?" he asked, his tone emotionless. That left her nervous.

"He does not know." Shame washed through her. Hearing her explain her actions made her realize she looked as wretched as her actions were.

Wolfe tipped up her chin and she read pity in his eyes. "I'm sorry I placed you in that situation, Kate. You do not bear this weight and choice alone. It is mine also. I should have known something was amiss after hearing of your betrothal. I should have known a woman in love with one man, could not do an about face and love another so quickly." He paused, shaking his head. "I do not pretend not to be slighted that you would marry another, have Saville raise my child as his own, possibly an heir. I would be lying if I said I were not hurt by that, but I do understand."

Kate swallowed the lump in her throat, hating the choice she made. "I should have written to you. I'm so sorry, Wolfe. I just couldn't bring myself to trapping you into a marriage in that way, but I suppose I thought to trap Saville into one in any case, so I'm a wretched person."

"You are not a wretched person. Do not ever say that."

"So you forgive me?" she asked, praying he would.

"I forgive you, of course. There is no harm done, not now that I'm here." He brushed his lips against hers. "I'm sorry it took me so long to know my own mind, but I'm not leaving. Not now or ever."

He slipped the ring onto her left hand. Kate stared at the promise it portrayed, its beauty beyond anything she'd ever known. "Forever?" she asked.

"And ever," he replied.

EPILOGUE

Kennech Hall, Derbyshire, one month later

Wolfe ran his hand over Kate's stomach, the little round bauble that grew daily a miracle he'd forever marvel over.

"That tickles," she said, smiling and running her hand through his hair.

He put his ear to her belly but could not hear anything but a little gurgling. "Is that you or the baby?" he asked.

She laughed and pushed him away. "We've not had breakfast yet, and I'm famished."

"Hmm, I'm famished too. For you." He came over her, enjoying that she slept naked after their lovemaking the night before. "How is my duchess this morning?"

She slipped her legs around his waist and pulled him close. His cock hardened, and he adjusted himself, needing her with a madness that never seemed to dim.

Her warm, welcoming body maddened him, and he

groaned at their joining, wanting to pleasure her in all ways, sex merely one of them.

"She requires her husband." She reached for him, pulling him down for a kiss. The embrace deepened, igniting a fire that would not be cooled within them. He took her then and gave her what they both wanted. His mind reeled at how perfect his life was. How happy and complete to have her and their little family in Derbyshire. A family that would equal four in a matter of months.

"I love you. So much," he said.

She pushed on his shoulder, and he rolled to his back. Kate came over him, settling on his cock and riding him from atop. Her breasts rocked with each stroke, and he reached for them, so perfect and heavy in his hands.

Just as she was his and he was hers.

He rolled her nipples between his fingers, and she moaned. "I cannot get enough of you," she admitted, her ministrations on top of him becoming frantic.

Over the last month, Kate's appetite was more feverish than he'd ever known. Not that he was complaining, and when he had whispered such concerns to the doctor, the elderly gentleman had stated that sometimes women experienced a higher drive toward sexual conduct.

The news had calmed any of his concerns and amused him in turn. His wife was a little vixen, and he could not have adored this side of her more than he already did.

He took a deep breath, his balls tightening when she rode him relentlessly, bringing him close to climax. He felt the first tremors of her release and watched, devouring the sight of her coming apart in his arms.

Wolfe let go of his control and arrived with her, reveling in the exquisite pleasure she brought to his bed and life.

Never a man alive was as fortunate as he was.

How he adored her.

She collapsed onto his chest, her breathing labored, and he pulled her close, running his hand along her spine. "Are you satisfied, Your Grace? I have all day if you wish to go another round," he teased.

She chuckled and reached for her nightgown thrown at the end of the bed. "No, we must get up. Do not forget you're to give Oliver his first riding lesson today. He's quite excited."

He lay in the bed, leaning on one arm, and watched as Kate slipped from him and went over to the bellpull, ringing for her maid. "I have not forgotten. In fact, I've had a new pony brought from London. He's a sweet thirteen hands and almost twenty years of age. He will not have any feistiness in him that could make riding dangerous. Oliver is, after all, only two."

"True, and I thank you for your care with him."

Wolfe sat up, gesturing for her to return. She yielded, and he pulled her into his arms. "There is no thanks needed. I love your son as much as I will love our child growing in your belly. I will raise him with you, ensure he learns all there is to know to be a strong and good earl. He will want for nothing, just as you will want for nothing. Do not thank me for being Oliver's father. It is a position I treasure and I will not disappoint you."

Kate's eyes filled with tears, another trait the doctor stated was typical and common with pregnant mothers. She wrapped her arms around his neck and held him tight.

"Sometimes I wake at night in a panic that all this is a dream. That I made a terrible error of judgment and married Saville."

Wolfe shuddered, not even wanting to imagine such a horror. "But you did not, my love. You married me, and there is no escaping me now."

"I do not want to," she whispered into his ear.

"Neither do I."

DON'T MISS TAMARA'S OTHER ROMANCE SERIES

The Wayward Yorks

A Wager with a Duke

My Reformed Rogue

Wild, Wild, Duke

In the Duke of Time

Duke Around and Find Out

The Wayward Woodvilles

A Duke of a Time

On a Wild Duke Chase

Speak of the Duke

Every Duke has a Silver Lining

One Day my Duke Will Come

Surrender to the Duke

My Reckless Earl

Brazen Rogue

The Notorious Lord Sin

Wicked in My Bed

League of Unweddable Gentlemen

Tempt Me, Your Grace

Hellion at Heart

Dare to be Scandalous

To Be Wicked With You

Kiss Me, Duke

The Marquess is Mine

Kiss the Wallflower

A Midsummer Kiss

A Kiss at Mistletoe

A Kiss in Spring

To Fall For a Kiss

A Duke's Wild Kiss

To Kiss a Highland Rose

To Marry a Rogue

Only an Earl Will Do

Only a Duke Will Do

Only a Viscount Will Do

Only a Marquess Will Do

Only a Lady Will Do

Lords of London

To Bedevil a Duke

To Madden a Marquess

To Tempt an Earl

To Vex a Viscount

To Dare a Duchess

To Marry a Marchioness

Royal House of Atharia

To Dream of You

About the Author

Tamara is an Australian author who grew up in an old mining town in country South Australia, where her love of history was founded. So much so, she made her darling husband travel to the UK for their honeymoon, where she dragged him from one historical monument and castle to another.

A mother of three, her two little gentlemen in the making, a future lady (she hopes) keep her busy in the real world, but whenever she gets a moment's peace she loves to write romance novels in an array of genres, including regency, medieval and time travel.